SF
Bova
   Exiles; 3 novellas

COPY 1

Exiles

Exiles

3 Novellas
edited by
Ben Bova

(.)

St. Martin's Press
New York

Library of Congress Cataloging in Publication Data
Main entry under title:

Exiles: 3 novellas.

CONTENTS: Anderson, P. Gypsy.—Russell, E. F. And
then there were none.—Asimov, I. Profession.
1. Science fiction, American. I. Bova, Benjamin.
II. Anderson, Poul, 1926- Gypsy. 1978.
III. Russell, Eric Frank, 1905- And then there were
none. 1978. IV. Asimov, Isaac, 1920- Profession.
1978.
PZ1.E936 [PS648.S3] 813'.0876 78-3974
ISBN 0-312-27493-9

CONTENTS

INTRODUCTION

I have been trying for several weeks to figure out how *not* to write this introduction. Procrastination is nothing new to writers, but this is not procrastination. It's a moral dilemma.

The idea of Futura Publications' and St. Martin's Press's THREE BY series is to present the best science fiction novellas ever written, in books that are easily accessible to the average reader. The novella — a story that ranges in length from 15,000 to 30,000 words — very often disappears from the literary scene after its first printing in a magazine or author's collection of stories. Novellas are of an awkward length: too short to stand in their own as individual books; too long to be easily included in anthologies.

How does this lead to a moral dilemma? Patience, please.

The THREE BY series brings us three fine science fiction novellas in each book. Each story is by one of the best authors in the science fiction field. In many cases, these stories have become 'classics', but because of their difficult lengths they have not been as widely anthologized as shorter (and often lesser) works.

Selecting the best science fiction novellas ever written is a happy task. Introducing them is quite another matter. I decided right from the start that the stories should stand by themselves, and speak for themselves. As an American President once said, it is 'far above our poor power to add or detract' from these stories. Let critics search out the hidden meanings in each tale; let teachers split hairs as to whether this certain story is a distopian vision or 'merely' (!) a rousing adventure. To introduce each volume in the THREE BY series, I would far rather talk about the field of science fiction, or about the authors themselves than about their stories.

Which brings us to my moral dilemma.

I have known Poul Anderson for many years, but our friendship has been confined to occasional short visits. He lives on the west coast of the U.S., I live on the east coast. We are colleagues, and friends. I admire the man and his work hugely. But we are not *close* friends, alas.

Worse still, I have never met Eric Frank Russell, never corresponded with him, never known him in any way except by reading his marvellous science fiction stories.

But worst of all (and here is the crux of the matter) I have known Isaac Asimov for just about twenty years, longer than I have known any other writer. He is as close to me as a brother. We have shared many trials, and millions of laughs.

So, at the risk of boring you and embarrassing Isaac, this introduction is going to be mostly about Asimov.

Mostly.

I do want to say one small, but perhaps important, thing about Poul Anderson and Eric Frank Russell. They are two of the most *undervalued* writers that this field has ever seen. They have produced great bodies of work that have brought year upon year of pleasure to millions of readers. Almost unnoticed by the fashionable critics and teachers of SF, they have turned out a rich stream of innovative, entertaining, thought-provoking stories – such as *Gypsy* and *And Then There Were None* – stories that will still be entertaining readers and making them think (which is what science fiction is all about) long after this year's stylistic wonderworks have sunk into that special oblivion that's reserved for books that have nothing to say.

And perhaps that's what's so special about Anderson and Russell. They have something to say. Story after story, year after year, they constantly tickle, tease, and surprise us by challenging our ideas, by appealing to our intellect, by forcing us to *think*.

Undervalued, that's what they are. But not unappreciated.

Now about Isaac . . .

I first met him in the late fifties at (where else?) a science fiction convention. Within a couple of years we were neighbours – at least we both lived in suburban Boston. I phoned him once to ask a question about biochemistry, and he was kind enough to visit me and spend an evening pouring detailed information into my head – between jokes.

Not long after that I received a phone call from him. He said:

'Cele Goldsmith (the editor of *Amazing* magazine at that time) is going to call you and ask you to do a series of articles

8

about life on other worlds.'

My response was something on the order of, 'Huh?'

'She wanted me to do the series but I can't; I'm too busy. I told her you would do it, and that you knew more about the subject than I do.'

'You told her *what?*'

'Listen, listen. Here's what I mean. Whatever I know, you'll know. All you have to do is ask. And you're bound to know some things that I don't – so you know more about it than I do!'

Typical Asimovian logic. And it worked. Whenever I was stuck, I asked Isaac. He never stinted of time or effort to help me.

Over the years Isaac has thrown so many opportunities my way that I've often considered giving him the ten per cent commissions that my erstwhile agents take out of assignments that Isaac has earned for me. Whenever I tell him that I'm thinking – just *thinking* of it, mind you – Isaac laughs.

'Listen,' he says, 'when I recommend you for something, I can be sure that it's going to be done well enough so that I don't have to change my name and leave town.'

Full of praise, he is.

We went through divorces more or less simultaneously, he remorseful with Jewish guilt, me burdened with the Catholic imitation of it. During this time we happened to be together on a cruise ship, from which we witnessed the Apollo 17 launch as the guests of the Holland-America Line. One dinner-time, Isaac said mournfully:

'Our ex-wives up in Massachusetts must think we're jet-setting around the world in the lap of luxury.'

We were sitting in the ship's beautiful dining saloon, partaking of our fourth meal of the day, accompanied by the women we loved.

'Isaac,' I said, 'we are!'

It never occurred to him. No matter where he is, Isaac's inner being is still in the candy store in Brooklyn where he grew up.

There are many tales of Isaac's prodigious output of books. As this is being written, he's working on his two-hundredth: his autobiography.

The evening after Isaac and his second wife, Dr Janet Jeppson, moved from their separate apartments to a spiffy new penthouse, my new wife and I took them out to dinner. Walking back along the midtown Manhattan streets, we passed the building that Isaac had just vacated.

He was instantly nostalgic. Looking up at his old window, he said, with a tear in his voice, 'It wasn't such a bad place. I was there fifty-six months and I wrote fifty-six books.'

I fainted.

A few months ago, Isaac suffered a very mild coronary, the most widely publicized illness in North America since Babe Ruth's famous bellyache of 1925. While he was confined to a hospital bed, I took over a few speaking engagements for him.

'Don't be too good,' he told me, 'or they'll never invite me back again.'

I assured him that he was in no danger. And he wasn't. But after appearing at a luncheon as his 'summer replacement', I got a phone call from Issac.

'I just wanted to apologize,' he said.

'For what?'

'For putting you to all this trouble.'

It was the first time I'd received an apology from a coronary victim for having his heart attack.

In summary, Issac is a man of contrasts. Despite a brash exterior, he is still a wide-eyed boy from Brooklyn. Although he loves to pinch young ladies (and older ladies, too) he is really a gentleman in the truest sense of that word. A self-admitted genius, he is also the warmest-hearted man I know.

And, believe it or not, despite his phenomenal success as a writer, Isaac often belittles his literary achievements. 'I couldn't write good,' he's said many times, 'so I've written a lot.'

Which is utter nonsense, as his story, *Profession*, in this volume amply demonstrates.

He does write a lot, and very well. He may be something of an ecological menace because his many books require whole forests of trees to be turned into paper. But, to paraphrase some pundit's estimation of him: 'He is a natural resource and an international treasure.'

And a good and true friend.

GYPSY

by Poul Anderson

Colonists to the far stars must have built-in yearning for the far horizon – the desire to go back of beyond. Some of them, though, may have too much.

From afar, I caught a glimpse of the *Traveller* as my boat swung towards the planet. The great spaceship looked like a toy at that distance, a frail bubble of metal and air and energy against the enormous background of space. I thought of the machines within her, humming and whirring and clicking very faintly as they pursued their unending round of services, making that long hull into a living world – the hull that was now empty of life – and I had a sudden odd feeling of sympathy. As if she were alive, I felt that the *Traveller* was lonely.

The planet swelled before me, a shining blue shield blazoned with clouds and continents, rolling against a limitless dark and the bitterly burning stars. Harbour, we had named that world, the harbour at the end of our long journey, and there were few lovelier names. Harbour, haven, rest and peace and a sky overhead as roof against the naked blaze of space. It was good to get home.

I searched the heavens, for another glimpse of the *Traveller*, but I couldn't find her tiny form in that thronging wilderness of stars. No matter, she was still on her orbit about Harbour, moored to the planet, perhaps for ever. I concentrated on bringing the spaceboat down.

Atmosphere whistled about the hull. After a month in the gloom and poisonous cold of the fifth planet, alone among utterly unhuman natives, I was usually on fire to get home and brought my craft down with a recklessness that overloaded the gravity beams. But this time I went a little more carefully, telling myself that I'd rather be late for supper than not arrive at all. Or perhaps it was that brief chance vision of the *Traveller* which made me suddenly thoughtful. After all, we had had some good times aboard her.

I sent the boat slanting towards the peninsula in the north temperate zone on which most of us were settled. The outraged air screamed behind me as I slammed down on the hard-packed earth that served us for a landing field. There were a few warehouses and service shops around it, long low buildings of the heavy timbers used by most of the colonists, and a couple of private homes a kilometre or so away. But otherwise only long grass rustled in the wind, gardens and wild groves, sunlight streaming out of a high blue sky. When I stepped from the boat, the fresh vivid scent of the land fairly leaped to meet me. I could hear the sea growling beyond the horizon.

Tokogama was on duty at the field. He was sitting on the porch of the office, smoking his pipe and watching the clouds sail by overhead, but he greeted me with the undemonstrative cordiality of old friends who know each other too well to need many words.

'So that's the portmaster,' I said. 'Soft touch. All you have to do is puff that vile-smelling thing and say hello to me.'

'That's all,' he admitted cheerfully. 'I am retained only for my uncommonly high ornamental value.'

It was, approximately, true. Our aircraft used the field with no formality, and we only kept this one space vessel in operation. The portmaster was on hand simply to oversee servicing and in the unlikely case of some emergency or dispute. But none of the colony's few public posts – captain, communications officer, and the rest – required much effort in as simple a society as ours, and they were filled as spare-time occupations by anyone who wanted them. There was no compensation except getting first turn at using the machinery for farming or heavy construction which we owned in common.

'How was the trip?' asked Tokogama.

'Pretty good,' I said. 'I gave them our machines and they filled my holds with their ores and alloys. And I managed to take a few more notes on their habits, and establish a few more code symbols for communication.'

'Which is a very notable brick added to the walls of science, but in view of the fact that you're the only one who ever goes there it really makes no odds.' Tokogama's dark eyes regarded me curiously. 'Why do you keep on making those trips out there, Erling? Quite a few of the other boys wouldn't mind visiting Five once in a while. Will and Ivan both mentioned it to me last week.'

'I'm no hog,' I said. 'If either of them, or anyone else, wants a turn at the trading job, let 'em learn space piloting and they can go. But meanwhile – I like the work. You know that. I was one of those who voted to continue the search for Earth.'

Tokogama nodded. 'So you were. But that was three years ago. Even you must have grown some roots here.'

'Oh, I have,' I laughed. 'Which reminds me I'm hungry, and judging by the sun it's the local dinner time. So I'll get on home, if Alanna knows I'm back.'

'She can't help it,' he smiled. 'The whole continent knows when you're back, the way you rip the atmosphere coming in. That home cooking must have a powerful magnetic attraction.'

'A steak aroma of about fifty thousand gauss – ' I turned to go, calling over my shoulder: 'Why don't you come to dinner tomorrow evening? I'll invite the other boys and we'll have an old-fashioned hot air session.'

'I was sort of hinting in that direction,' said Tokogama.

I got my carplane out of the hangar and took off with a whisper of air and a hum of grav-beam generators. But I flew low over the woods and meadows, dawdling along at fifty kilometres an hour and looking across the landscape. It lay quietly in the evening, almost empty of man, a green fair breadth of land veined with bright rivers. The westering sun touched each leaf and grass blade with molten gold, an aureate glow which seemed to fill the cool air like a tangible presence, and I could hear the chirp and chatter of the great bird flocks as they settled down in the trees. Yes – it was good to get home.

My own house stood at the very edge of the sea, on a sandy bluff sloping down to the water. The windy trees which grew about it almost hid the little stone and timber structure, but its lawns and gardens reached far, and beyond them were the fields from which we got our food. Down by the beach stood the boathouse and the little dock I had made, and I knew our sailboat lay waiting there for me to take her out. I felt an almost physical hunger for the sea again, the mighty surge of waves out to the wild horizon, the keen salt wind and the crying white birds. After a month in the sterile tanked air of the spaceboat, it was like being born again.

I set the plane down before the house and got out. Two small bodies fairly exploded against me – Einar and Mike. I walked into the house with my sons riding my shoulders.

Alanna stood in the doorway waiting for me. She was tall, almost as tall as I, and slim and red-haired and the most beautiful woman in the universe. We didn't say much – it was unnecessary, and we were otherwise occupied for the next few minutes.

And afterwards I sat before a leaping fire where the little flames danced and chuckled and cast a wavering ruddy glow over the room, and the wind whistled outside and rattled the door, and the sea roared on the nighted beach, and I told them of my fabulous space voyage, which had been hard and monotonous and lonely but was a glamorous adventure at home. The boys' eyes never stirred from my face as I talked, I could feel the eagerness that blazed from them. The gaunt sun-seared crags of One, the misty jungles of Two, the mountains and deserts of Four, the great civilization of Five, the bitter desolation of the outer worlds – and beyond those the stars. But we were home now, we sat in a warm dry house and heard the wind singing outside.

I was happy, in a quiet way that had somehow lost the exuberance of my earlier returns. Content, maybe.

Oh, well, I thought. These trips to the fifth world were becoming routine, just as life on Harbour, now that our colony was established and our automatic and semiautomatic machines running smoothly, had quieted down from the first great riot of work and danger and work again. That was progress, that was what we had striven for, to remove want and woe and the knife-edged uncertainty which had haunted our days. We had arrived, we had graduated into a solid assurance and a comfort which still held enough unsureness and challenge to keep us from getting sluggish. Grown men don't risk their necks climbing the uppermost branches of trees, the way children do; they walk on the ground, and when they have to rise they do so safely and comfortably, in a carplane.

'What's the matter, Erling?' asked Alanna.

'Why – nothing,' I started out of my reverie, suddenly aware that the children were in bed and the night near its middle. 'Nothing at all. I was just sitting thinking. A little tired, I guess. Let's turn in.'

'You're a poor liar, Erling,' she said softly. 'What were you really thinking about?'

'Nothing,' I insisted. 'That is, well, I saw the old *Traveller* as I was coming down today. It just put me in mind of old times.'

'It would,' she said. And suddenly she sighed. I looked at her in some alarm, but she was smiling again. 'You're right, it is late, and we'd better go to bed.'

I took the boys out in the sailboat the next day. Alanna stayed home on the excuse that she had to prepare dinner, though I knew of her theory that the proper psychodevelopment of children required a balance of paternal and maternal influence. Since I was away so much of the time, out in space or with one of the exploring parties which were slowly mapping our planet, she made me occupy the centre of the screen whenever I was home.

Einar, who was nine years old and getting interested in the microbooks we had from the *Traveller* – and so, ultimately, from Earth – looked at her and said: 'Back at Sol you wouldn't have to make food, Mother. You'd just set the au . . . autochef, and come out with us.'

'I like to cook,' she smiled. 'I suppose we could make autochefs, now that the more important semirobot machinery has been produced, but it'd take a lot of fun out of life for me.'

Her eyes went past the house, down to the beach and out over the restless sun-sparked water. The sea breeze ruffled her red hair, it was like a flame in the cool shade of the trees. 'I think they must miss a lot in the Solar System,' she said. 'They have so much there that, somehow, they can't have what we've got – room to move about, lands that never saw a man before, the fun of making something ourselves.'

'You might like it if you went there,' I said. 'After all, sweetheart, however wisely we may talk about Sol we know it only by hearsay.'

'I know I like what we have here,' she answered. I thought there was a faint note of defiance in her voice. 'If Sol is just a legend, I can't be sure I'd like the reality. Certainly it could be no better than Harbour.'

'All redheads are chauvinists,' I laughed, turning down towards the beach.

'All Swedes make unfounded generalizations,' she replied cheerfully. 'I should'a known better than to marry a Thorkild.'

'Fortunately, Mrs Thorkild, you didn't,' I bowed.

The boys and I got out the sailboat. There was a spanking breeze, and in minutes we were scudding northward, along the woods and fields and tumbling surf of the coast.

'We should put a motor on the *Naughty Nancy*, Dad,' said Einar. 'Suppose this wind don't hold.'

'I like to sail,' I said. 'The chance of having to man the sweeps is part of the fun.'

'Me too,' said Mike, a little ambiguously.

'Do they have sailboats on Earth?' asked Einar.

'They must,' I said, 'since I designed the *Nancy* after a book about them. But I don't think it'd ever be quite the same, Einar. The sea must always be full of boats, most of them powered, and there'd be aircraft overhead and some sort of building wherever you made landfall. You wouldn't have the sea to yourself.'

'Then why'd you want to keep looking for Earth when everybody else wanted to stay here?' he challenged.

A nine-year-old can ask some remarkably disconcerting questions. I said slowly: 'I wasn't the only one who voted to keep on searching. And – well, I admitted it at the time, it wasn't Earth but the search itself that I wanted. I liked to find new planets. But we've got a good home now, Einar, here on Harbour.'

'I still don't understand how they ever lost Earth,' he said.

'Nobody does,' I said. 'The *Traveller* was carrying a load of colonists to Alpha Centauri – that was a star close to Sol – and men had found the hyperdrive only a few years before and reached the nearer stars. Anyway, *something* happened. There was a great explosion in the engines, and we found ourselves somewhere else in the Galaxy, thousands of light-years from home. We don't know how far from home, since

16

we've never been able to find Sol again. But after repairing the ship, we spent more than twenty years looking. We never found home.' I added quickly, 'Until we decided to settle on Harbour. That was our home.'

'I mean, how'd the ship get thrown so far off?'

I shrugged. The principles of the hyperdrive are difficult enough, involving as they do the concept of multiple dimensions and of discontinuous psi functions. No one on the ship – and everyone with a knowledge of physics had twisted his brains over the problem – had been able to figure out what catastrophe it was that had annihilated space-time for her. Speculation had involved space warps – whatever that term means, points of infinite discontinuity, undimensional fields, and Cosmos knows what else. Could we find what had happened, and purposefully control the phenomenon which had seized us by some blind accident, the Galaxy would be ours. Meanwhile, we were limited to pseudovelocities of a couple of hundred lights, and interstellar space mocked us with vastness.

But how explain that to a nine-year-old? I said only: 'If I knew that, I'd be wiser than anyone else, Einar. Which I'm not.'

'I wanna go swimming,' said Mike.

'Sure,' I said. 'That was our idea, wasn't it? We'll drop anchor in the next bay – '

'I wanna go swimming in Spacecamp Cove.'

I tried to hedge, but Einar was all over me, too. It was only a few kilometres farther up the coast, and its broad sheltered expanse, its wide sandy beach and the forest immediately behind, made it ideal for such an expedition. And after all, I had nothing against it.

Nothing – except the lure of the place.

I sighed and surrendered. Spacecamp Cove it was.

We had a good time there, swimming and picnicking, playing ball and loafing in the sand and swimming some more. It was good to lie in the sun again, with a cool wet wind blowing in from the sea and talking in the trees. And to the boys, the glamour of it was a sort of crown on the day.

But I had to fight that romance. I wasn't a child any more, playing at spacemen and aliens, I was a grown man with some responsibilities. The community of the *Traveller* had voted by an overwhelming majority to settle on Harbour, and that was that.

And here, half hidden by long grass, half buried in the blowing sand, were the unmistakable signs of what we had left.

There wasn't much. A few plastic containers for food, a couple of broken tools of curious shape, some scattered engine parts. Just enough to indicate that a while ago – ten years ago, perhaps – a party of spacemen had landed here, camped for a while, made some repairs, and resumed their journey.

They weren't from the fifth planet. Those natives had never left their world, and even with the technological impetus we were giving them in exchange for their metals they weren't ever likely to, the pressures they needed to live were too great. They weren't from Sol, or even some colony world – not only were the remains totally unlike our equipment, but the news of a planet like Harbour, almost a duplicate of Earth but without a native intelligent race, would have brought settlers here in swarms. So – somewhere in the Galaxy, someone else had mastered the hyperdrive and was exploring space.

As we had been doing –

I did my best to be cheerful all the way home, and think I succeeded on the surface. And that in spite of Einar's wildly romantic gabble about the unknown campers. But I couldn't help remembering –

In twenty years of spacing, you can see a lot of worlds, and you can have a lot of experience. We had been gods of a sort, flitting from star to star, exploring, trading, learning, now and again mixing into the destinies of the natives. We had fought and striven, suffered and laughed and stood silent in wonder. For most of us, the dreadful hunger for home, the weariness of the hopeless quest, had shadowed that panorama of worlds which reeled through my mind. But – before Cosmos, I had loved every minute of it!

I fell into unrelieved moodiness as soon as we had stowed the *Naughty Nancy* in our boathouse. The boys ran ahead of me towards the house, but I followed slowly. Alanna met me at the door.

'Better wash up right away,' she said. 'The company will be here any minute.'

'Uh-huh.'

She looked at me, for a very long moment, and laid her hand on my arm. In the long dazzling rays of the westering sun, her eyes were brighter than I had seen them before. I wondered if tears were not wavering just behind them.

'You were at Spacecamp Cove,' she said quietly.

'The boys wanted to go there,' I answered. 'It's a good place.'

'Erling – ' She paused. I stood looking at her, thinking how beautiful she was. I remembered the way she had looked on Hralfar, the first time I kissed her. We had wandered a ways from the camp of the detail exploring that frosty little world and negotiating with its natives for supplies. The sky had been dark overhead, with a shrunken sun casting its thin pale light on the blue-shadowed snow. It was quiet, breathlessly quiet, the air was like sharp fire in our nostrils and her hair, the only colour in that white horizon, seemed to crackle with frost. That was quite a long time ago, but nothing had changed between us since.

'Yes?' I prompted her. 'Yes, what is it?'

Her voice came quickly, very low so the boys wouldn't hear: 'Erling, are you really happy here?'

'Why' – I felt an almost physical shock of surprise – 'of course I am, dear. That's a silly question.'

'Or a silly answer?' She smiled, with closed lips. 'We did have some good times on the *Traveller*. Even those who grumbled loudest at the time admit that, now when they've got a little perspective on the voyage and have forgotten something of the overcrowding and danger and weariness. But you – I sometimes think the *Traveller* was your life, Erling.'

'I liked the ship, of course.' I had a somewhat desperate sense of defending myself. 'After all, I was born and raised on her. I never really knew anything else. Our planetary visits were so short, and most of the worlds so unterrestrial. You liked it, too.'

'Oh, sure, it was fun to go batting around the Galaxy, never knowing what might wait at the next sun. But a woman wants a home. And – Erling, plenty of others your age, who also had never known anything else, hated it.'

'I was lucky. As an officer, I had better quarters, more privacy. And, well, that "something hid behind the ranges" maybe meant more to me than to most others. But – good Cosmos, Alanna! you don't think that now – '

'I don't think anything, Erling. But on the ship you weren't so absent-minded, so apt to fall into daydreams. You didn't sit around the place all day, you were always working on something – ' She bit her lip. 'Don't misunderstand, Erling. I have no doubt you keep telling yourself how happy you are. You could go to your cremation, here on Harbour, thinking you'd had a rather good life. But – I sometimes wonder!'

'Now look – ' I began.

'No, no, nothing more out of you. Get inside and wash up, the company'll be coming in half a minute.'

I went, with my head in a whirl. Mechanically, I scrubbed myself and changed into evening blouse and slacks. When I came out of the bedroom, the first of the guests were already waiting.

MacTeague Angus was there, the old first mate of the *Traveller* and captain in the short time between Kane's death and our settling on Harbour. So was my brother Thorkild Gustav, with whom I had little in common except a mutual liking. Tokogama Hideyoshi, Petroff Ivan, Ortega Manuel, and a couple of others showed up a few minutes later. Alanna took charge of their wives and children, and I mixed drinks all around.

For a while the talk was of local matters. We were scattered over quite a wide area, and had as yet not produced enough telescreens for every house, so that communication was limited to direct personal travel by plane. A hailstorm on Gustav's farm, a minor breakdown in the vehicle factory superintended by Ortega, Petroff's project of a fleet of semirobot fishing boats – small gossip. Presently dinner was served.

Gustav was rapturous over the steak. 'What is it?' he asked.

'Some local animal I shot the other day,' I said. 'Ungulate, reddish-brown, broad flat horns.'

'Oh, yes. Hm-m-m – I'll have to try domesticating some. I've had pretty good luck with those glug-gugs.'

'Huh?' Petroff stared at him.

'Another local species,' laughed Gustav. 'I had to call them something, and they make that kind of noise.'

'The *Traveller* was never like this,' said Ortega, helping himself to another piece of meat.

'I never thought the food was bad,' I said.

'No, we had the hydroponic vegetables and fruits, and the synthetic meats, as well as what we picked up on different planets,' admitted Ortega. 'But it wasn't this good, ever. Hydroponics somehow don't have the flavour of Earth-grown stuff.'

'That's your imagination,' said Petroff. 'I can prove – '

'I don't care what you can prove, the facts remain.' Ortega glanced at me. 'But there were compensations.'

'Not enough,' muttered Gustav. 'I've got room to move, here on Harbour.'

'You're being unjust to the *Traveller*,' I said. 'She was only meant to carry about fifty people, for a short voyage at that. When she lost her way for twenty years, and a whole new generation got jammed in with their parents, it's no wonder she grew crowded. Actually, her minimum crew is ten or so. Thirty people – fifteen couples, say, plus their kids – could travel in her in ease and comfort, with private apartments for all.'

'And still . . . still, for over twenty years, we fought and suffered and stood the monotony and the hopelessness – to find Earth.' Tokogama's voice was musing, a little awed. 'When all the time, on any of a hundred uninhabited terrestroid planets, we could have had – this.'

'For at least half that time,' pointed out MacTeague, 'we were simply looking for the right part of the Galaxy. We knew Sol wasn't anywhere near, so we had no hopes to be crushed, but we thought as soon as the constellations began to look fairly familiar we'd be quickly able to find home.' He shrugged. 'But space is simply too big, and our astrogational tables have so little information. Star travel was still in its infancy when we left Sol.

'An error of, say, one per cent could throw us light-years off in the course of several hundred parsecs. And the Galaxy is lousy with GO-type suns, which are statistically almost certain to have neighbours sufficiently like Sol's to fool an unsure observer. If our tables had given positions relative to, say, S Doradus, we could have found home easily enough. But they used Sirius for their bright-star point – and we couldn't find Sirius in that swarm of stars! We just had to hop from star to star which *might* be Sol – and find it wasn't, and go on, with the sickening fear that maybe we were getting farther away all the time, maybe Sol lay just off the bows, obscured by a dark nebula. In the end – we gave it up as a bad job.'

'There's more to it than that,' said Tokogama. 'We realized all that, you know. But there was Captain Kane and his tremendous personality, his driving will to success, and we'd all come to rely more or less blindly on him. As long as he lived, nobody quite believed in the possibility of failure. When he died, everything seemed to collapse at once.'

I nodded grimly, remembering those terrible days that followed – Seymour's mutinous attempt to seize power, bringing home to us just how sick and weary we all were; the arrival at this star which might have solved it all, might have given us a happy ending, if it had been Sol; the rest on Harbour, a rest which became a permanent stay –

'Something else kept us going all those years, too,' said Ortega quietly. 'There was an element among the younger generation which liked to wander. The vote to stay here wasn't unanimous.'

'I know,' said MacTeague. His level gaze rested thoughtfully on me. 'I often wonder, Erling, why some of you don't borrow the ship and visit the nearer stars, just to see what's there.'

'Wouldn't do any good,' I said tonelessly. 'It'd just make our feet itch worse than ever – and there'd always be stars beyond those.'

'But why –' Gustav fumbled for words. 'Why would anyone *want* to go – stargazing that way? I . . . well, I've got my feet on ground now, my own ground, my own home . . . it's growing, I'm building and planting and seeing it come to reality before my own eyes, and it'll be there for my children and their children. There's air and wind and rain, sunlight, the sea, the woods and mountains – Cosmos! Who wants more? Who wants to trade it for sitting in a sterile metal tank, riding from star to star, homeless, hopeless?'

'Nobody,' I said hastily. 'I was just trying – '

'The most pointless existence – simply to be a ... a spectator in the universe!'

'Not exactly,' said Tokogama. 'There was plenty we did, if you insist that somebody must do something. We brought some benefits of human civilization to quite a number of places. We did some extensive star-mapping, if we ever see Earthmen again they'll find our tables useful, and our observations within different systems. We . . . well, we were wanderers, but so what? Do you blame a bird for not having hoofs?'

'The birds have hoofs now,' I said. 'They're walking on the ground. And' – I flashed a glance at Alanna – 'they like it.'

The conversation was getting a little too hot. I steered it into safer channels until we adjourned to the living room. Over coffee and tobacco it came back.

We began reminiscing about the old days, planets we had seen, deeds we had done. Worlds and suns and moons, whirling through a raw dark emptiness afire with stars, were in our talk – strange races, foreign cities, lonely magnificence of mountains and plains and seas, the giant universe opening before us. Oh, by all the gods, we had fared far!

We had seen the blue hell-flames leaping over the naked peaks of a planet whose great sun almost filled its sky. We had sailed with a gang of happy pirates over a sea red as new-spilled blood towards the grotesque towers of a fortress older than their history. We had seen the rich colour and flashing metal of a tournament on Drangor and the steely immensity of the continental cities on Alkan. We had talked philosophy with a gross wallowing cephalopod on one world and been shot at by the inhumanly beautiful natives of another. We had come as gods to a planet to lift its barbaric natives from the grip of a plague that scythed them down and we had come as humble students to the ancient laboratories and libraries of the next. We had come near perishing in a methane storm on a planet far from its sun and felt then how dear life is. We had lain on the beaches of the paradise world Luanha and let the sea sing us to sleep. We had ridden centauroids who conversed with us as they went to the aerial city of their winged enemies –

More than the wildly romantic adventures – which, after all, had been pretty dirty and bloody affairs at the time – we loved to remember the worlds themselves: a fiery sunset on the snowfields of Hralfar; a great brown river flowing through the rain forest which covered Atlang; a painted desert on Thyvari; the mighty disc of New Jupiter swelling before our bows; the cold and vastness and cruelty and emptiness and awe and wonder of open space itself. And, in our small clique of frank tramps, there had been the comradeship of the road, the calm unspoken knowledge of having friends who would stand firm – a feeling of *belonging*, such as men like Gustav had achieved only since coming here, and which we seemed to have lost.

Lost – yes, why not admit it? We didn't see each other very often any more, we were too scattered, too busy. And the talk of the others was just a little bit boring.

Well, it couldn't be helped –

It was late that night when the party broke up. Alanna and I saw the guests out to their planes. When the last vehicle had whispered into the sky, we stood for a while looking around us. The night was very still and cool, with a high starry sky in which the moon of Harbour was rising. Its light glittered on the dew under our feet, danced restlessly on the sea, threw a dim silver veil on the dreaming land – our land.

I looked down at Alanna. She was staring over the darkened view, staring as if she had never seen it before – or never would again. The moonlight was tangled like frost in her hair. *What if I never see open space again? What if I sit here till I die? This is worth it.*

She spoke at last, very slowly, as if she had to shape each word separately: 'I'm beginning to realize it. Yes, I'm quite sure.'

'Sure of what?' I asked.

'Don't play dumb. You know what I mean. You and Manuel and Ivan and Hideyoshi and the others who were here – except Angus and Gus, of course. And quite a few more. You don't belong here. None of you.'

'How – so?'

'Look, a man who had been born and raised in a city, and had a successful life in it, couldn't be expected to take to the

24

country all of a sudden. Maybe never. Put him among peasants, and he'd go around all the rest of his life wondering vaguely why he wasn't honestly happy.'

'We – Now don't start that again, sweetheart,' I begged.

'Why not? Somebody's got to. After all, Erling, this is a peasantry we've got, growing up on Harbour. More or less mechanized, to be sure, but still rooted to the soil, close to it, with the peasant strength and solidity and the peasant's provincial outlook. Why, if a ship from Earth landed tomorrow, I don't think twenty people would leave with it.

'But you, Erling, you and your friends – you grew up in the ship, and you made a successful adaptation to it. You spent your formative years wandering. By now – you're cosmopolites. For you, a mountain range will always be more than it really is, because of what's behind it. One horizon isn't enough, you've got to have many, as many as there are in the universe.

'Find Earth? Why, you yourself admitted you don't care whether Earth is ever found. You want only the search.

'You're a gypsy, Erling. And no gypsy could ever be tied to one place.'

I stood for a long while, alone with her in the cold calm moonlight, and said nothing. When I looked down at her, finally, she was trying not to cry, but her lip was trembling and the tears were bright in her eyes. Every word was wrenched out of me:

'You may be right, Alanna. I'm beginning to be horribly afraid you are. But what's to be done about it?'

'Done?' She laughed, a strangely desolate laugh. 'Why, it's a very simple problem. The answer is circling right there up in the sky. Get a crew who feel the way you do, and take the *Traveller*. Go roaming – for ever!'

'But . . . you? You, the kids, the place here . . . you – '

'Don't you see?' Her laughter rang louder now, echoing faintly in the light night. 'Don't you see? I want to go, too!' She almost fell into my arms. 'I want to go, too!'

There is no reason to record the long arguments, grudging acceptances, slow preparations. In the end we won. Sixteen men and their wives, with half a dozen children, were wild to leave.

That summer blazed up into fall, winter came, spring, and summer again, while we made ready. Our last year on Harbour. And I had never realized how much I loved the planet. Almost, I gave up.

But space, free space, the open universe and the ship come alive again –

We left the colony a complete set of plans, in the unlikely event that they should ever want to build a starship of their own, and a couple of spaceboats and duplicates of all the important automatic machinery carried by the *Traveller*. We would make astrogating tables, as our official purpose, and theoretically we might some day come back.

But we knew we never would. We would go travelling, and our children would carry the journey on after us, and their children after them, a whole new civilization growing up between the stars, rootless but tremendously alive. Those who wearied of it could always colonize a planet, we would be spreading mankind over the Galaxy. When our descendants were many, they would build other ships until there was a fleet, a mobile city hurtling from sun to sun. It would be a culture to itself, drawing on the best which all races had to offer and spreading it over the worlds. It would be the bloodstream of the interstellar civilization which was slowly gestating in the universe.

As the days and months went by, my boys grew ever more impatient to be off. I smiled a little. Right now, they only thought of the adventure of it, romantic planets and great deeds to be done. Well, there were such, they would have eventful lives, but they would soon learn that patience and steadfastness were needed, that there was toil and suffering and danger – and life!

Alanna – I was a little puzzled. She was very gay when I was around, merrier than I had ever seen her before. But she often went out for long walks, alone on the beach or in the sun-dappled woods, and she started a garden which she would never harvest. Well – so it went, and I was too busy with preparations to think much about it.

The end came, and we embarked on the long voyage, the voyage which has not ceased yet and, I hope, will never end. The night before, we had Angus and Gustav in for a farewell party, and it was a strange feeling to be saying goodbye knowing that we would never see them again, or hear from them. It was like dying.

But we were alone in the morning. We went out to our carplane, to fly to the landing field where the gypsies would meet. From there, a boat would take us to the *Traveller*. I still could not fully realize that I was captain – I, captain of the great ship which had been my world, it didn't seem real. I walked slowly, my head full of the sudden universe of responsibility.

Alanna touched my arm. 'Look around, Erling,' she whispered. 'Look around at our land. You'll never see it again.'

I shook myself out of my reverie and let my eyes sweep the horizon. It was early, the grass was still wet, flashing in the new sun. The sea danced and glittered beyond the rustling trees, crying its old song to the fair green land, and the wind that blew from it was keen and cold and pungent with life. The fields were stirring in the wind, a long ripple of grass, and high overhead a bird was singing.

'It's – very beautiful,' I said.

'Yes.' I could hardly hear her voice. 'Yes, it is. Let's go, Erling.'

We got into the carplane and slanted skyward. The boys crowded forward with me, staring ahead for the first glimpse of the landing field, not seeing the forests and meadows and shining rivers that slipped away beneath us.

Alanna sat behind me, looking down over the land. Her bright head was bent away so I couldn't see her face. I wondered what she was thinking, but somehow I didn't want to ask her.

... AND THEN THERE WERE NONE

by Eric Frank Russell

The battleship was eight hundred feet in diameter and slightly more than one mile long. Mass like that takes up room and makes a dent. This one sprawled right across one field and halfway through the next. Its weight was a rut twenty feet deep which would be there for keeps.

On board were two thousand people divisible into three distinct types. The tall, lean, crinkly-eyed ones were the crew. The crop-haired, heavy-jowled ones were the troops. Finally, the expressionless, balding and myopic ones were the cargo of bureaucrats.

The first of these types viewed this world with the professional but aloof interest of people everlastingly giving a planet the swift onceover before chasing along to the next. The troops regarded it with a mixture of tough contempt and boredom. The bureaucrats peered at it with cold authority. Each according to his lights.

This lot were accustomed to new worlds, had dealt with them by the dozens and reduced the process to mere routine. The task before them would have been nothing more than repetition of well-used, smoothly operating technique but for one thing: the entire bunch were in a jam and did not know it.

Emergence from the ship was in strict order of precedence. First, the Imperial Ambassador. Second, the battleship's captain. Third, the officer commanding the ground forces. Fourth, the senior civil servant.

Then, of course, the next grade lower, in the same order: His Excellency's private secretary, the ship's second officer, the deputy commander of troops, the penultimate pen-pusher.

Down another grade, then another, until there was left only His Excellency's barber, boot wiper and valet, crew members with the lowly status of O.S. – Ordinary Spaceman – the military nonentities in the ranks, and a few temporary ink-pot fillers dreaming of the day when they would be made permanent and given a desk of their own. This last collection of unfortunates remained aboard to clean ship and refrain from smoking, by command.

Had this world been alien, hostile and well-armed, the order of exit would have been reversed, exemplifying the Biblical promise that the last shall be first and the first shall be last. But this planet, although officially new, unofficially was not new and certainly was not alien. In ledgers and dusty files some two hundred light-years away it was recorded as a cryptic number and classified as a ripe plum long overdue for picking. There had been considerable delay in the harvesting due to a superabundance of other still riper plums elsewhere.

According to the records, this planet was on the outermost fringe of a huge assortment of worlds which had been settled immediately following the Great Explosion. Every school child knew all about the Great Explosion, which was no more than the spectacular name given to the bursting outward of masses of humanity when the Blieder drive superseded atomic-powered rockets and practically handed them the cosmos on a platter.

At that time, between three and five hundred years ago, every family, group, cult or clique that imagined it could do better some place else had taken to the star trails. The restless, the ambitious, the malcontents, the eccentrics, the antisocial, the fidgety and the just plain curious, away they had roared by the dozens, the hundreds, the thousands.

Some two hundred thousand had come to this particular world, the last of them arriving three centuries back. As usual, ninety per cent of the mainstream had consisted of friends, relatives or acquaintances of the first-comers, people persuaded to follow the bold example of Uncle Eddie or Good Old Joe.

If they had since doubled themselves six or seven times over, there now ought to be several millions of them. That they had increased far beyond their original strength had been evident during the approach, for while no great cities were visible there were many medium to smallish towns and a large number of villages.

His Excellency looked with approval at the turf under his feet, plucked a blade of it, grunting as he stooped. He was so constructed that this effort approximated to an athletic feat and gave him a crick in the belly.

'Earth-type grass. Notice that, captain? Is it just a coincidence, or did they bring seed with them?'

'Coincidence, probably,' said Captain Grayder. 'I've come across four grassy worlds so far. No reason why there shouldn't be others.'

'No, I suppose not.' His Excellency gazed into the distance, doing it with pride of ownership. 'Looks like there's someone ploughing over there. He's using a little engine between a pair of fat wheels. They can't be so backward. Hm-m-m!' He rubbed a couple of chins. 'Bring him here. We'll have a talk, find out where it's best to get started.'

'Very well.' Captain Grayder turned to Colonel Shelton, boss of the troops. 'His Excellency wishes to speak to that farmer.' He pointed to the faraway figure.

'The farmer,' said Shelton to Major Hame. 'His Excellency wants him at once.'

'Bring that farmer here,' Hame ordered Lieutenant Deacon. 'Quickly!'

'Go get that farmer,' Deacon told Sergeant-Major Bidworthy. 'And hurry – His Excellency is waiting!'

The sergeant-major, a big, purple-faced man, sought around for a lesser rank, remembered that they were all cleaning ship and not smoking. He, it seemed, was elected.

Tramping across four fields and coming within hailing distance of his objective, he performed a precise military halt and released a barracks-square bellow of, 'Hi, you!' He waved urgently.

The farmer stopped, wiped his forehead, looked around. His manner suggested that the mountainous bulk of the battleship was a mirage such as are five a penny around these parts. Bidworthy waved again, making it an authoritative summons. The farmer calmly waved back, got on with his ploughing.

Sergeant-Major Bidworthy employed an expletive which – when its flames had died out – meant, 'Dear me!' and marched fifty paces nearer. He could now see that the other was bushy-browed and leather-faced.

'*Hi!*'

Stopping the plough again, the farmer leaned on a shaft, picked his teeth.

Struck by the notion that perhaps during the last three centuries the old Earth-language had been dropped in favour of some other lingo, Bidworthy asked, 'Can you understand me?'

'Can any person understand another?' inquired the farmer, with clear diction. He turned to resume his task.

Bidworthy was afflicted with a moment of confusion. Recovering, he informed hurriedly, 'His Excellency, the Earth Ambassador, wishes to speak with you at once.'

'So?' The other eyed him speculatively. 'How come that he is excellent?'

'He is a person of considerable importance,' said Bidworthy, unable to decide whether the other was being funny at his expense or alternatively was what is known as a character. A good many of these isolated planet-scratchers liked to think of themselves as characters.

'Of considerable importance,' echoed the farmer, narrowing his eyes at the horizon. He appeared to be trying to grasp an alien concept. After a while, he inquired, 'What will happen to your home world when this person dies?'

'Nothing,' Bidworthy admitted.

'It will roll on as usual?'

'Of course.'

'Then,' declared the farmer, flatly, 'he cannot be important.' With that, his little engine went *chuff-chuff* and the wheels rolled forward and the plough ploughed.

Digging his nails into the palms of his hands, Bidworthy spent half a minute gathering oxygen before he said, in hoarse tones, 'I cannot return without at least a message for His Excellency.'

'Indeed?' The other was incredulous. 'What is to stop you?' Then, noting the alarming increase in Bidworthy's colour, he added with compassion, 'Oh, well, you may tell him that I said' – he paused while he thought it over – 'God bless you and goodbye!'

Sergeant-Major Bidworthy was a powerful man who weighed two hundred and twenty pounds, had hopped around the cosmos for twenty years, and feared nothing. He had never been known to permit the shiver of one hair – but he was trembling all over by the time he got back to the ship.

His Excellency fastened a cold eye upon him and demanded, 'Well?'

'He won't come.' Bidworthy's veins stood out on his forehead. 'And, sir, if only I could have him in my field company for a few months I'd straighten him up and teach him to move at the double.'

'I don't doubt that, sergeant-major,' soothed His Excellency. He continued in a whispered aside to Colonel Shelton. 'He's a good fellow but no diplomat. Too abrupt and harsh voiced. Better go yourself and fetch that farmer. We can't sit here forever waiting to find out where to begin.'

'Very well, Your Excellency.' Colonel Shelton trudged across the fields, caught up with the plough. Smiling pleasantly, he said, 'Good morning, my man!'

Stopping his plough, the farmer sighed as if it were another of those days one has sometimes. His eyes were dark-brown, almost black, as they looked at the other.

'What makes you think I'm *your* man?' he inquired.

'It's a figure of speech,' explained Shelton. He could see what was wrong now, Bidworthy had fallen foul of an irascible type. Two dogs snarling at one another. Shelton went on. 'I was only trying to be courteous.'

'Well,' meditated the farmer, 'I reckon that's something worth trying for.'

Pinking a little, Shelton continued with determination. 'I am commanded to request the pleasure of your company at the ship.'

'Think they'll get any pleasure out of my company?' asked the other, disconcertingly bland.

'I'm sure of it,' said Shelton.

'You're a liar,' said the farmer.

His colour deepening, Colonel Shelton snapped, 'I do not permit people to call me a liar.'

'You've just permitted it,' the other pointed out.

Letting it pass, Shelton insisted, 'Are you coming to the ship or are you not?'

'I am not.'

'Why not?'

'Myob!' said the farmer.

'What was that?'

'Myob?' he repeated. It smacked of a mild insult.

Colonel Shelton went back.

He told the ambassador, 'That fellow is one of these too-clever types. All I could get out of him at the finish was "myob", whatever that means.'

'Local slang,' chipped in Captain Grayder. 'An awful lot of it develops over three or four centuries. I've come across one or two worlds where there's been so much of it that one almost had to learn a new language.'

'He understood your speech?' asked the ambassador, looking at Shelton.

'Yes, Your Excellency. And his own is quite good. But he won't come away from his ploughing.' He reflected briefly, then suggested, 'If it were left to me, I'd bring him in by force, under an armed escort.'

'That would encourage him to give essential information,' commented the ambassador, with open sarcasm. He patted his stomach, smoothed his jacket, glanced down at his glossy shoes. 'Nothing for it but to go speak to him myself.'

Colonel Shelton was shocked. 'Your Excellency, you can't do *that!*'

'Why can't I?'

'It would be undignified.'

'I am aware of it,' said the ambassador, dryly. 'Can you suggest an alternative?'

'We can send out a patrol to find someone more co-operative.'

'Someone better informed, too,' Captain Grayder offered. 'At best we wouldn't get much out of one surly hayseed. I doubt whether he knows a quarter of what we require to learn.'

'All right.' His Excellency abandoned the notion of doing his own chores. 'Organize a patrol and let's have some results.'

'A patrol,' said Colonel Shelton to Major Hame. 'Nominate one immediately.'

'Call out a patrol,' Hame ordered Lieutenant Deacon. 'At once.'

'Parade a patrol forthwith, sergeant-major,' said Deacon.

Bidworthy went to the ship, climbed a ladder, stuck his

head in the lock and bawled, 'Sergeant Gleed, out with your squad, and make it snappy!' He gave a suspicious sniff and went farther into the lock. His voice gained several more decibels. 'Who's been smoking? By the Black Sack, if I catch – '

Across the fields something quietly went *chuff-chuff* while balloon tyres crawled along.

The patrol formed by the right in two ranks of eight men each, turned at a barked command, marched off noseward. Their boots thumped in unison, their accoutrements clattered and the orange-coloured sun made sparkles on their metal.

Sergeant Gleed did not have to take his men far. They had got one hundred yards beyond the battleship's nose when he noticed a man ambling across the field to his right. Treating the ship with utter indifference, the newcomer was making towards the farmer still ploughing far over to the left.

'Patrol, right wheel!' yelled Gleed. Marching them straight past the wayfarer, he gave them a loud about-turn and followed it with the high-sign.

Speeding up its pace, the patrol opened its ranks, became a double file of men tramping at either side of the lone pedestrian. Ignoring his suddenly acquired escort, the latter continued to plod straight ahead like one long convinced that all is illusion.

'Left wheel!' Gleed roared, trying to bend the whole caboodle towards the waiting ambassador.

Swiftly obedient, the double file headed leftward, one, two, three, hup! It was neat, precise execution, beautiful to watch. Only one thing spoiled it: the man in the middle maintained his self-chosen orbit and ambled casually between numbers four and five of the right-hand file.

That upset Gleed, especially since the patrol continued to thump ambassadorwards for lack of a further order. His Excellency was being treated to the unmilitary spectacle of an escort dumbly boot-beating one way while its prisoner airily mooched another. Colonel Shelton would have plenty to say about it in due course, and anything he forgot Bidworthy would remember.

'Patrol!' hoarsed Gleed, pointing an outraged finger at the escapee, and momentarily dismissing all regulation commands from his mind. 'Get that yimp!'

34

Breaking ranks, they moved at the double and surrounded the wanderer too closely to permit further progress. Perforce, he stopped.

Gleed came up, said somewhat breathlessly, 'Look, the Earth Ambassador wants to speak to you – that's all.'

The other said nothing, merely gazed at him with mild blue eyes. He was a funny-looking bum, long overdue for a shave, with a fringe of ginger whiskers sticking out all around his pan. He resembled a sunflower.

'Are you going to talk with His Excellency?' Gleed persisted.

'Naw.' The other nodded towards the farmer. 'Going to talk with Zeke.'

'The ambassador first,' retorted Gleed, toughly. 'He's a big noise.'

'I don't doubt that,' remarked the sunflower.

'Smartie Artie, eh?' said Gleed, pushing his face close and making it unpleasant. He gave his men a gesture. 'All right – shove him along. We'll show him!'

Smartie Artie sat down. He did it sort of solidly, giving himself the aspect of a statue anchored for aeons. The ginger whiskers did nothing to lend grace to the situation. But Sergeant Gleed had handled sitters before, the only difference being that this one was cold sober.

'Pick him up,' ordered Gleed, 'and carry him.'

They picked him up and carried him, feet first, whiskers last. He hung limp and unresisting in their hands, a dead weight. In this inauspicious manner he arrived in the presence of the Earth Ambassador where the escort plonked him on his feet.

Promptly he set out for Zeke.

'Hold him, darn you!' howled Gleed.

The patrol grabbed and clung tight. His Excellency eyed the whiskers with well-bred concealment of distaste, coughed delicately, and spoke.

'I am truly sorry that you had to come to me in this fashion.'

'In that case,' suggested the prisoner, 'you could have saved yourself some mental anguish by not permitting it to happen.'

'There was no other choice. We've got to make contact somehow.'

'I don't see it,' said Ginger Whiskers. 'What's so special about this date?'

'The date?' His Excellency frowned in puzzlement. 'Where does that come in?'

'That's what I'd like to know.'

'The point eludes me.' The ambassador turned to Colonel Shelton. 'Do you get what he's aiming at?'

'I could hazard a guess, Your Excellency. I think he is suggesting that since we've left them without contact for more than three hundred years, there's no particular urgency about making it today.' He looked at the sunflower for confirmation.

That worthy rallied to his support by remarking, 'You're doing pretty well for a half-wit.'

Regardless of Shelton's own reaction, this was too much for Bidworthy purpling near by. His chest came up and his eyes caught fire. His voice was an authoritative rasp.

'Be more respectful while addressing high-ranking officers!'

The prisoner's mild blue eyes turned upon him in childish amazement, examined him slowly from feet to head and all the way down again. The eyes drifted back to the ambassador.

'Who is this preposterous person?'

Dismissing the question with an impatient wave of his hand, the ambassador said, 'See here, it is not our purpose to bother you from sheer perversity, as you seem to think. Neither do we wish to detain you any longer than is necessary. All we – '

Pulling at his face-fringe as if to accentuate its offensiveness, the other interjected, 'It being you, of course, who determines the length of the necessity?'

'On the contrary, you may decide that yourself,' said the ambassador, displaying admirable self-control. 'All you need do is tell – '

'Then I've decided it right now,' the prisoner chipped in. He tried to heave himself free of his escort. 'Let me go talk to Zeke.'

'All you need do,' the ambassador persisted, 'is to tell us where we can find a local official who can put us in touch with your central government.' His gaze was stern, commanding, as he added, 'For instance, where is the nearest police post?'

'Myob!' said the other.

'The same to you,' retorted the ambassador, his patience starting to evaporate.

'That's precisely what I'm trying to do,' assured the prisoner, enigmatically. 'Only you won't let me.'

'If I may make a suggestion, Your Excellency,' put in Colonel Shelton, 'let me – '

'I require no suggestions and I won't let you,' said the ambassador, rapidly becoming brusque. 'I have had enough of all this tomfoolery. I think we've landed at random in an area reserved for imbeciles and it would be as well to recognize the fact and get out of it with no more delay.'

'Now you're talking,' approved Ginger Whiskers. 'And the farther the better.'

'I'm not thinking of leaving this planet if that's what is in your incomprehensible mind,' asserted the ambassador, with much sarcasm. He stamped a proprietory foot on the turf. 'This is part of the Earth Empire. As such, it is going to be recognized, charted and organized.'

'*Heah, heah !*' put in the senior civil servant, who aspired to honours in elocution.

His Excellency threw a frown behind, went on, 'We'll move the ship to some other section where brains are brighter.' He signed to the escort. 'Let him go. Doubtless he is in a hurry to borrow a razor.'

They released their grips. Ginger Whiskers at once turned towards the still-ploughing farmer, much as if he were a magnetized needle irresistibly drawn Zekeward. Without a word he set off at his original mooching pace. Disappointment and disgust showed on the faces of Gleed and Bidworthy as they watched him go.

'Have the vessel shifted at once,' the ambassador instructed Captain Grayder. 'Plant it near a suitable town – not out in the wilds where every hayseed views strangers as a bunch of gyps.'

He marched importantly up the gangway. Captain Grayder followed, then Colonel Shelton, then the elocutionist. Next their successors in due order of precedence. Lastly, Gleed and his men.

The gangway rolled inward. The lock closed. Despite its

37

immense bulk, the ship shivered briefly from end to end and soared without deafening uproar or spectacular display of flame.

Indeed, there was silence save for the plough going *chuff-chuff* and the murmurings of the two men walking behind it. Neither bothered to turn his head to observe what was happening.

'Seven pounds of prime tobacco is a heck of a lot to give for one case of brandy,' Ginger Whiskers was protesting.

'Not for my brandy,' said Zeke. 'It's stronger than a thousand Gans and smoother than an Earthman's downfall.'

The great battleship's second touchdown was made on a wide flat one mile north of a town estimated to hold twelve to fifteen thousand people. Captain Grayder would have preferred to survey the place from low altitude before making his landing, but one cannot manoeuvre an immense space-going job as if it were an atmospheric tug. Only two things can be done so close to a planetary surface – the ship is taken up or brought down with no room for fiddling between times.

So Grayder bumped his ship in the best spot he could find when finding is a matter of split-second decisions. It made a rut only twelve feet deep, the ground being harder and on a rock bed. The gangway was shoved out; the procession descended in the same order as before.

His Excellency cast an anticipatory look towards the town, registered disappointment and remarked, 'Something's badly out of kilter here. There's the town. Here's us in plain view, with a ship like a metal mountain. A thousand people at least must have seen us even if the rest are holding seances behind drawn curtains or playing pinochle in the cellars. Are they excited?'

'It doesn't seem so,' admitted Colonel Shelton, pulling an eyelid for the sake of feeling it spring back.

'I wasn't asking you. I was telling you. They are not excited. They are not surprised. In fact, they are not even interested. One would almost think they've had a ship here before and it was full of smallpox, or sold them a load of gold bricks, or something like that. What is wrong with them?'

'Possibly they lack curiosity,' Shelton offered.

'Either that or they're afraid. Or maybe the entire gang of

them are crackers. A good many worlds were appropriated by woozy groups who wanted some place where their eccentricities could run loose. Nutty notions become conventional after three hundred years of undisturbed continuity. It's then considered normal and proper to nurse the bats out of your grandfather's attic. That, and generations of inbreeding, can create some queer types. But we'll cure 'em!'

'Yes, Your Excellency, most certainly we will.'

'You don't look so balanced yourself, chasing that eye around your pan,' reproved the ambassador. He pointed southeast as Shelton stuck the fidgety hand firmly into a pocket. 'There's a road over there. Wide and well-built by the looks of it. Get that patrol across it. If they don't bring in a willing talker within reasonable time, we'll send a battalion into the town itself.'

'A patrol,' repeated Colonel Shelton to Major Hame.

'Call out the patrol,' Hame ordered Lieutenant Deacon.

'That patrol again, sergeant-major,' said Deacon.

Bidworthy raked out Gleed and his men, indicated the road, barked a bit, shooed them on their way.

They marched, Gleed in the lead. Their objective was half a mile and angled slightly nearer the town. The left-hand file, who had a clear view of the nearest suburbs, eyed them wistfully, wished Gleed in warmer regions with Bidworthy stoking beneath him.

Hardly had they reached their goal than a customer appeared. He came from the town's outskirts, zooming along at fast pace on a contraption vaguely resembling a motorcycle. It ran on a pair of big rubber balls and was pulled by a caged fan. Gleed spread his men across the road.

The oncomer's machine suddenly gave forth a harsh, penetrating sound that vaguely reminded them of Bidworthy in the presence of dirty boots.

'Stay put,' warned Gleed. 'I'll skin the guy who gives way and leaves a gap.'

Again the shrill metallic warning. Nobody moved. The machine slowed, came up to them at a crawl and stopped. Its fan continued to spin at low rate, the blades almost visible and giving out a steady hiss.

'What's the idea?' demanded the rider. He was lean-featured, in his middle thirties, wore a gold ring in his nose and had a pigtail four feet long.

Blinking incredulously at this get-up, Gleed managed to jerk an indicative thumb towards the iron mountain and say, 'Earth ship.'

'Well, what d'you expect me to do about it?'

'Co-operate,' said Gleed, still bemused by the pigtail. He had never seen one before. It was in no way effeminate, he decided. Rather did it lend a touch of ferocity like that worn – according to the picture books – by certain North American aborigines of umpteen centuries ago.

'Co-operation,' mused the rider. 'Now there is a beautiful word. You know what it means, of course?'

'I ain't a dope.'

'The precise degree of your idiocy is not under discussion at the moment,' the rider pointed out. His nose-ring waggled a bit as he spoke. 'We are talking about co-operation. I take it you do quite a lot of it yourself?'

'You bet I do,' Gleed assured. 'And so does everyone else who knows what's good for him.'

'Let's keep to the subject, shall we? Let's not sidetrack and go rambling all over the map.' He revved up his fan a little then let it slow down again. 'You are given orders and you obey them?'

'Of course. I'd have a rough time if – '

'That is what you call co-operation?' put in the other. He shrugged his shoulders, indulged a resigned sigh. 'Oh, well, it's nice to check the facts of history. The books *could* be wrong.' His fan flashed into a circle of light and the machine surged forward. 'Pardon me.'

The front rubber ball barged forcefully between two men, knocking them sidewise without injury. With a high whine, the machine shot down the road, its fan-blast making the rider's plaited hairdo point horizontally backward.

'You goofy glumps!' raged Gleed as his fallen pair got up and dusted themselves. 'I ordered you to stand fast. What d'you mean, letting him run out on us like that?'

'Didn't have much choice about it, sarge,' answered one, giving him a surly look.

'I want none of your back-chat. You could have busted a

balloon if you'd had your weapons ready. That would have stopped him.'

'You didn't tell us to have guns ready.'

'Where was your own, anyway?' added a voice.

Gleed whirled round on the others and bawled, 'Who said that?' His irate eyes raked a long row of blank, impassive faces. It was impossible to detect the culprit. 'I'll shake you up with the next quota of fatigues,' he promised. 'I'll see to it –'

'The sergeant-major's coming,' one of them warned.

Bidworthy was four hundred yards away and making martial progress towards them. Arriving in due time, he cast a cold, contemptuous glance over the patrol.

'What happened?'

Giving a brief account of the incident, Gleed finished aggrievedly, 'He looked like a Chicasaw with an oil well.'

'What's a Chicasaw?' Bidworthy demanded.

'I read about them somewhere once when I was a kid,' explained Gleed, happy to bestow a modicum of learning. 'They had long haircuts, wore blankets and rode around in gold-plated automobiles.'

'Sounds crazy to me,' said Bidworthy. 'I gave up all that magic-carpet stuff when I was seven. I was deep in ballistics before I was twelve and military logistics at fourteen.' He sniffed loudly, gave the other a jaundiced eye. 'Some guys suffer from arrested development.'

'They actually existed,' Gleed maintained. 'They – '

'So did fairies,' snapped Bidworthy. 'My mother said so. My mother was a good woman. She didn't tell me a lot of tomfool lies – often.' He spat on the road. 'Be your age!' Then he scowled at the patrol. 'All right, get out your guns, assuming that you've got them and know where they are and which hand to hold them in. Take orders from me. I'll deal personally with the next one along.'

He sat on a large stone by the roadside and planted an expectant gaze on the town. Gleed posed near him, slightly pained. The patrol remained strung across the road, guns held ready. Half an hour crawled by without anything happening.

One of the men said, 'Can we have a smoke, sergeant-major?'

'No.'

They fell into lugubrious silence, watching the town, licking their lips and thinking. They had plenty to think about. A town – any town of human occupation – had desirable features not found elsewhere in the cosmos. Lights, company, freedom, laughter, all the makings of life. And one can go hungry too long.

Eventually a large coach came from the outskirts, hit the high road, came bowling towards them. A long, shiny, streamlined job, it rolled on twenty balls in two rows of ten, gave forth a whine similar to but louder than that of its predecessor, but had no visible fans. It was loaded with people.

At a point two hundred yards from the road block a loudspeaker under the vehicle's bonnet blared an urgent, 'Make way! Make way!'

'This is it,' commented Bidworthy, with much satisfaction. 'We've got a dollop of them. One of them is going to chat or I leave the service.' He got off his rock, stood in readiness.

'Make way! Make way!'

'Bust his bags if he tries to bull his way through,' Bidworthy ordered the men.

It wasn't necessary. The coach lost pace, stopped with its bonnet a yard from the waiting file. Its driver peered out the side of his cab. Other faces snooped farther back.

Composing himself and determined to try the effect of fraternal cordiality, Bidworthy went up to the driver and said, 'Good morning.'

'Your time-sense is shot to pot,' observed the other. He had a blue jowl, a broken nose, cauliflower ears, looked the sort who usually drives with others in hot and vengeful pursuit. 'Can't you afford a watch?'

'Huh?'

'It isn't morning. It's late afternoon.'

'So it is,' admitted Bidworthy, forcing a cracked smile. 'Good afternoon.'

'I'm not so sure about that,' mused the driver, leaning on his wheel and moodily picking his teeth. 'It's just another one nearer the grave.'

'That may be,' agreed Bidworthy, little taken with that ghoulish angle. 'But I have other things to worry about, and – '

'Not much use worrying about anything, past or present,' advised the driver. 'Because there are lots bigger worries to come.'

'Perhaps so,' Bidworthy said, inwardly feeling that this was no time or place to contemplate the darker side of existence. 'But I prefer to deal with my own troubles in my own time and my own way.'

'Nobody's troubles are entirely their own, nor their time, nor their methods,' remarked the tough-looking oracle. 'Are they now?'

'I don't know and I don't care,' said Bidworthy, his composure thinning down as his blood pressure built up. He was conscious of Gleed and the patrol watching, listening, and probably grinning inside themselves. There was also the load of gaping passengers. 'I think you are chewing the fat just to stall me. You might as well know now that it won't work. The Earth Ambassador is waiting – '

'So are we,' remarked the driver, pointedly.

'He wants to speak to you,' Bidworthy went on, 'and he's going to speak to you!'

'I'd be the last to prevent him. We've got free speech here. Let him step up and say his piece so's we can get on our way.'

'*You*,' Bidworthy informed, 'are going to *him*.' He signed to the rest of the coach. 'And your load as well.'

'Not me,' denied a fat man, sticking his head out of a side window. He wore thick-lensed glasses that gave him eyes like poached eggs. Moreover, he was adorned with a high hat candy-striped in white and pink. 'Not me,' repeated this vision, with considerable firmness.

'Me, neither,' endorsed the driver.

'All right,' Bidworthy registered menace. 'Move this birdcage an inch, forward or backward, and we'll shoot your potbellied tyres to thin strips. Get out of that cab.'

'Not me. I'm too comfortable. Try fetching me out.'

Bidworthy beckoned to his nearest six men. 'You heard him – take him up on that.'

Tearing open the cab door, they grabbed. If they had expected the victim to put up a futile fight against heavy odds, they were disappointed. He made no attempt to resist. They

43

got him, lugged together, and he yielded with good grace, his body leaning sidewise and coming halfway out of the door.

That was as far as they could get him.

'Come on,' urged Bidworthy, displaying impatience. 'Show him who's who. He isn't a fixture.'

One of the men climbed over the body, poked around inside the cab, and said, 'He is, you know.'

'What d'you mean?'

'He's chained to the steering column.'

'Eh! Let me see.' He had a look, found that it was so. A chain and a small but heavy and complicated padlock linked the driver's leg to his coach. 'Where's the key?'

'Search me,' invited the driver grinning.

They did just that. The frisk proved futile. No key.

'Who's got it?'

'Myob!'

'Shove him back into his seat,' ordered Bidworthy, looking savage. 'We'll take the passengers. One yap's as good as another so far as I'm concerned.' He strode to the doors, jerked them open. 'Get out and make it snappy.'

Nobody budged. They studied him silently and with varied expressions, not one of which did anything to help his ego. The fat man with the candy-striped hat mooned at him sardonically. Bidworthy decided that he did not like the fat man and that a stiff course of military calisthenics might thin him down a bit.

'You can come out on your feet,' he suggested to the passengers in general and the fat man in particular, 'or on your necks. Whichever you prefer. Make up your minds.'

'If you can't use your head you can at least use your eyes,' commented the fat man. He shifted in his seat to the accompaniment of metallic clanking noises.

Bidworthy did as suggested, leaning through the doors to have a gander. Then he got right into the vehicle, went its full length and studied each passenger. His florid features were two shades darker when he came out and spoke to Sergeant Gleed.

'They're all chained. Every one of them.' He glared at the driver. 'What's the big idea, manacling the lot?'

'Myob!' said the driver, airily.

44

'Who's got the keys?'

'Myob!'

Taking a deep breath, Bidworthy said to nobody in particular, 'Every so often I hear of some guy running amok and laying 'em out by the dozens. I always wonder why – but now I know.' He gnawed his knuckles, then added to Gleed, 'We can't run this contraption to the ship with that dummy blocking the driver's seat. Either we must find the keys or get tools and cut them loose.'

'Or you could wave us on our way and go take a pill,' offered the driver.

'Shut up! If I'm stuck here another million years I'll see to it that – '

'The colonel's coming,' muttered Gleed, giving him a nudge.

Colonel Shelton arrived, walked once slowly and officiously around the outside of the coach, examining its construction and its occupants. He flinched at the striped hat whose owner leered at him through the glass. Then he came over to the disgruntled group.

'What's the trouble this time, sergeant-major?'

'They're as crazy as the others, sir. They give a lot of lip and say, "Myob!" and couldn't care less about His Excellency. They don't want to come out and we can't get them out because they're chained to their seats.'

'Chained?' Shelton's eyebrows shot upward. 'What for?'

'I don't know, sir. They're linked in like a load of lifers making for the pen, and – '

Shelton moved off without waiting to hear the rest. He had a look for himself, came back.

'You may have something there, sergeant-major. But I don't think they are criminals.'

'No, sir?'

'No.' He threw a significant glance towards the colourful headgear and several other sartorial eccentricities, including a ginger-haired man's foot-wide polka-dotted bow. 'It is more likely that they're a bunch of whacks being taken to a giggle emporium. I'll ask the driver.' Going to the cab, he said, 'Do you mind telling me your destination?'

'Yes,' responded the other.

'Very well, where is it?'

'Look,' said the driver, 'are we talking the same language?'

'Huh?'

'You asked me if I minded and I said yes.' He made a gesture. 'I do mind.'

'You refuse to tell?'

'Your aim's improving, sonny.'

'Sonny?' put in Bidworthy, vibrant with outrage. 'Do you realize you are speaking to a colonel?'

'Leave this to me,' insisted Shelton, waving him down. His expression was cold as he returned his attention to the driver. 'On your way. I'm sorry you've been detained.'

'Think nothing of it,' said the driver, with exaggerated politeness. 'I'll do as much for you some day.'

With that enigmatic remark, he let his machine roll forward. The patrol parted to make room. The coach built up its whine to top note, sped down the road, diminished into the distance.

'By the Black Sack!' swore Bidworthy, staring purple-faced after it. 'This planet has got more punks in need of discipline than any this side of – '

'Calm yourself, sergeant-major,' advised Shelton. 'I feel the same way as you – but I'm taking care of my arteries. Blowing them full of bumps like seaweed won't solve any problems.'

'Maybe so, sir, but – '

'We're up against something mighty funny here,' Shelton went on. 'We've got to find out exactly what it is and how best to cope with it. That will probably mean new tactics. So far, the patrol has achieved nothing. It is wasting its time. We'll have to devise some other and more effective method of making contact with the powers-that-be. March the men back to the ship, sergeant-major.'

'Very well, sir.' Bidworthy saluted, swung around, clicked his heels, opened a cavernous mouth. 'Patro-o-ol! . . . right form!'

The conference lasted well into the night and halfway through the following morning. During these argumentative hours various oddments of traffic, mostly vehicular, passed along the road, but nothing paused to view the monster spaceship, nobody approached for a friendly word with its crew. The strange inhabitants of this world seemed to be afflicted with a peculiar form of mental blindness, unable to see a thing until it was thrust into their faces and then surveying it squint-eyed.

One passer-by in midmorning was a truck whining on two dozen rubber balls and loaded with girls wearing colourful head-scarves. The girls were singing something about one little kiss before we part, dear. Half a dozen troops lounging near the gangway came eagerly to life, waved, whistled and yoohooed. The effort was wasted, for the singing continued without break or pause and nobody waved back.

To add to the discomfiture of the love-hungry, Bidworthy stuck his head out of the lock and rasped, 'If you monkeys are bursting with surplus energy, I can find a few jobs for you to do – nice dirty ones.' He seared them one at a time before he withdrew.

Inside, the top brass sat around a horseshoe table in the chartroom near the bow and debated the situation. Most of them were content to repeat with extra emphasis what they had said the previous evening, there being no new points to bring up.

'Are you certain,' the Earth Ambassador asked Captain Grayder, 'that this planet has not been visited since the last emigration transport dumped the final load three hundred years back?'

'Positive, your excellency. Any such visit would have been recorded.'

'If made by an Earth ship. But what about others? I feel it in my bones that at some time or other these people have fallen foul of one or more vessels calling unofficially and have been leery of spaceships ever since. Perhaps somebody got tough with them, tried to muscle in where he wasn't wanted. Or they've had to beat off a gang of pirates. Or they were swindled by some unscrupulous fleet of traders.'

'Quite impossible, your excellency,' declared Grayder. 'Emigration was so scattered over so large a number of worlds that even today every one of them is under-populated, only one-hundredth developed, and utterly unable to build space-

47

ships of any kind, even rudimentary ones. Some may have the techniques but not the facilities, of which they need plenty.'

'Yes, that's what I've always understood.'

'All Blieder-drive vessels are built in the Sol system, registered as Earth ships and their whereabouts known. The only other ships in existence are eighty or ninety antiquated rocket jobs bought at scrap price by the Epsilon system for haulage work between their fourteen closely-planned planets. An old-fashioned rocket job couldn't reach this place in a hundred years.'

'No, of course not.'

'Unofficial boats capable of this range just don't exist,' Grayder assured. 'Neither do space buccaneers, for the same reason. A Blieder-job takes so much that a would-be pirate has to become a billionaire to become a pirate.'

'Then,' said the ambassador, heavily, 'back we go to my original theory – that something peculiar to this world plus a lot of inbreeding has made them nutty.'

'There's plenty to be said for that notion,' put in Colonel Shelton. 'You should have seen the coachload I looked over. There was a mortician wearing odd shoes, one brown, one yellow. And a moon-faced gump sporting a hat made from the skin of a barber's pole, all stripy. Only thing missing was his bubble pipe – and probably he'll be given that where he was going.'

'Where was he going?'

'I don't know, your excellency. They refused to say.'

Giving him a satirical look, the ambassador remarked, 'Well, that is a valuable addition to the sum total of our knowledge. Our minds are now enriched by the thought that an anonymous individual may be presented with a futile object for an indefinable purpose when he reaches his unknown destination.'

Shelton subsided, wishing that he had never seen the fat man, or, for that matter, the fat man's cockeyed world.

'Somewhere they've got a capital, a civic seat, a centre of government wherein function the people who hold the strings,' the ambassador asserted. 'We've got to find that place before we can take over and reorganize on up-to-date lines whatever setup they've got. A capital is big by the standards of its own

48

administrative area. It's never an ordinary, nondescript place. It has certain physical features lending it importance above the average. It should be easily visible from the air. We must make a search for it – in fact, that's what we ought to have done in the first place. Other planets' capital cities have been found without trouble. What's the hoodoo on this one?'

'See for yourself, your excellency.' Captain Grayder poked a couple of photographs across the table. 'There are the two hemispheres as recorded by us when coming in. They reveal nothing resembling a superior city. There isn't even a town conspicuously larger than its fellows or possessing outstanding features setting it apart from the others.'

'I don't place great faith in pictures, particularly when taken at long distance. The naked eye sees more. We have got four lifeboats capable of scouring the place from pole to pole. Why not use them?'

'Because, your excellency, they were not designed for such a purpose.'

'Does that matter so long as they get results?'

Grayder said, patiently, 'They were designed to be launched in space and hit up to forty thousand. They are ordinary, old-style rocket jobs, for emergencies only. You could not make efficient ground-survey at any speed in excess of four hundred miles per hour. Keep the boats down to that and you're trying to run them at landing-speed, muffling the tubes, balling up their efficiency, creating a terrible waste of fuel, and inviting a crash which you're likely to get before you're through.'

'Then it's high time we had Blieder-drive lifeboats on Blieder-drive ships.'

'I agree, your excellency. But the smallest Blieder engine has an Earth mass of more than three hundred tons – far too much for little boats.' Picking up the photographs, Grayder slid them into a drawer. 'What we need is an ancient, propeller-driven airplane. They could do something we can't do – they could go slow.'

'You might as well yearn for a bicycle,' scoffed the ambassador, feeling thwarted.

'We have a bicycle,' Grayder informed. 'Tenth Engineer Harrison owns one.'

49

'And he has brought it with him?'

'It goes everywhere with him. There is a rumour that he sleeps with it.'

'A spaceman toting a bicycle!' The ambassador blew his nose with a loud honk. 'I take it that he is thrilled by the sense of immense velocity it gives him, an ecstatic feeling of rushing headlong through space?'

'I wouldn't know, your excellency.'

'Hm-m-m! Bring this Harrison in to me. We'll set a nut to catch a nut.'

Grayder blinked, went to the caller board, spoke over the ship's system. 'Tenth Engineer Harrison wanted in the chartroom immediately.'

Within ten minutes Harrison appeared. He had walked fast three-quarters of a mile from the Blieder room. He was thin and wiry, with dark, monkeylike eyes, and a pair of ears that cut out the pedalling with the wind behind him. The ambassador examined him curiously, much as a zoologist would inspect a pink giraffe.

'Mister, I understand that you possess a bicycle.'

Becoming wary, Harrison said, 'There's nothing against it in the regulations, sir, and therefore – '

'Darn the regulations!' The ambassador made an impatient gesture. 'We're stalled in the middle of a crazy situation and we're turning to crazy methods to get moving.'

'I see, sir.'

'So I want you to do a job for me. Get out your bicycle, ride down to town, find the mayor, sheriff, grand panjandrum, supreme galootie, or whatever he's called, and tell him he's officially invited to evening dinner along with any other civic dignitaries he cares to bring and, of course, their wives.'

'Very well, sir.'

'Informal attire,' added the ambassador.

Harrison jerked up one ear, drooped the other, and said, 'Beg pardon, sir?'

'They can dress how they like.'

'I get it. Do I go right now, sir?'

'At once. Return as quickly as you can and bring me the reply.'

Saluting sloppily, Harrison went out. His Excellency found

an easy-chair, reposed in it at full length and ignored the others' stares.

'As easy as that!' He pulled out a long cigar, carefully bit off its end. 'If we can't touch their minds, we'll appeal to their bellies.' He cocked a knowing eye at Grayder. 'Captain, see that there is plenty to drink. Strong stuff. Venusian cognac or something equally potent. Give them an hour at a well-filled table and they'll talk plenty. We won't be able to shut them up all night.' He lit the cigar, puffed luxuriously. 'That is the tried and trusted technique of diplomacy – the insidious seduction of the distended gut. It always works – you'll see.'

Pedalling briskly down the road, Tenth Engineer Harrison reached the first street on either side of which were small detached houses with neat gardens front and back. A plump, amiable-looking woman was clipping a hedge halfway along. He pulled up near to her, politely touched his cap.

"Scuse me, ma'am, I'm looking for the biggest man in town.'

She half-turned, gave him no more than a casual glance, pointed her clipping-shears southward. 'That'd be Jeff Baines. First on the right, second on the left. It's a small delicatessen.'

'Thank you.'

He moved on, hearing the *snip-snip* resume behind him. First on the right. He curved around a long, low, rubber-balled truck parked by the corner. Second on the left. Three children pointed at him and yelled shrill warnings that his back wheel was going round. He found the delicatessen, propped a pedal on the kerb, gave his machine a reassuring pat before he went inside and had a look at Jeff.

There was plenty to see. Jeff had four chins, a twenty-two-inch neck, and a paunch that stuck out half a yard. An ordinary mortal could have got into either leg of his pants without taking off a diving suit. He weighed at least three hundred and undoubtedly *was* the biggest man in town.

'Wanting something?' inquired Jeff, lugging it up from far down.

'Not exactly.' Tenth Engineer Harrison eyed the succulent food display, decided that anything unsold by nightfall was not given to the cats. 'I'm looking for a certain person.'

'Are you now? Usually I avoid that sort – but every man to his taste.' He plucked at a fat lip while he mused a moment, then suggested, 'Try Sid Wilcock over on Dane Avenue. He's the most certain man I know.'

'I didn't mean it that way,' said Harrison. 'I meant I was searching for somebody particular.'

'Then why the dub didn't you say so?' Jeff Baines worked over the new problem, finally offered, 'Tod Green ought to fit that bill. You'll find him in the shoeshop end of this road. He's particular enough for anyone. He's downright finicky.'

'You misunderstand me,' Harrison explained. 'I'm hunting a bigwig so's I can invite him to a feed.'

Resting himself on a high stool which he overlapped by a foot all round, Jeff Baines eyed him peculiarly and said, 'There's something lopsided about this. In the first place, you're going to use up a considerable slice of your life finding a guy who wears a wig, especially if you insist on a big one. And where's the point of dumping an ob on him just because he uses a bean-blanket?'

'Huh?'

'It's plain common sense to plant an ob where it will cancel an old one out, isn't it?'

'Is it?' Harrison let his mouth hang open while his mind moiled around the strange problem of how to plant an ob.

'So you don't know?' Jeff Baines massaged a plump chop and sighed. He pointed at the other's middle. 'Is that a uniform you're wearing?'

'Yes.'

'A genuine, pukka, dyed-in-the-wool uniform?'

'Of course.'

'Ah!' said Jeff. 'That's where you've fooled me – coming in by yourself, on your ownsome. If there had been a gang of you dressed identically the same, I'd have known at once it was a uniform. That's what uniform means – all alike. Doesn't it?'

'I suppose so,' agreed Harrison, who had never given it a thought.

'So you're off that ship. I ought to have guessed it in the first place. I must be slow on the uptake today. But I didn't expect to see one, just one, messing around on a pedal contraption. It goes to show, doesn't it?'

'Yes,' said Harrison, glancing around to make sure that no confederate had swiped his bicycle while he was detained in conversation. The machine was still there. 'It goes to show.'

'All right, let's have it – what have you come here for ?'

'I've been trying to tell you all along. I've been sent to – '

'Been sent ?' Jeff's eyes widened a little. 'Mean to say you actually let yourself be *sent* ?'

Harrison gaped at him. 'Of course. Why not ?'

'Oh, I get it now,' said Jeff Baines, his puzzled features suddenly clearing. 'You confuse me with the queer way you talk. You mean you planted an ob on someone ?'

Desperately, Harrison said, 'What's an ob ?'

'He doesn't know,' commented Jeff Baines, looking prayerfully at the ceiling. 'He doesn't even know that!' He gave out a resigned sigh. 'You hungry by any chance ?'

'Going on that way.'

'OK. I could tell you what an ob is, but I'll do something better – I'll show you.' Heaving himself off the stool, he waddled to a door at back. 'Don't know why I should bother to try to educate a uniform. It's just that I'm bored. C'mon, follow me.'

Obediently, Harrison went behind the counter, paused to give his bicycle a reassuring nod, trailed the other through a passage and into a yard.

Jeff Baines pointed to a stack of cases. 'Canned goods.' He indicated an adjacent store. 'Bust 'em open and pile the stuff in there. Stack the empties outside. Please yourself whether you do it or not. That's freedom, isn't it ?' He lumbered back into the shop.

Left by himself, Harrison scratched his ears and thought it over. Somewhere, he felt, there was an obscure sort of gag. A candidate named Harrison was being tempted to qualify for his sucker certificate. But if the play was beneficial to its organizer it might be worth learning because the trick could then be passed on. One must speculate in order to accumulate.

So he dealt with the cases as required. It took him twenty minutes of brisk work, after which he returned to the shop.

'Now,' explained Baines, 'you've done something for me. That means you've planted an ob on me. I don't thank you for what you've done. There's no need to. All I have to do is get rid of the ob.'

'Ob?'

'Obligation. Why use a long word when a short one is good enough? An obligation is an ob. I shift it this way: Seth Warburton, next door but one, has got half a dozen of my ob saddled on him. So I get rid of mine to you and relieve him of one of his to me by sending you around for a meal.' He scribbled briefly on a slip of paper. 'Give him this.'

Harrison stared at it. In casual scrawl, it read, 'Feed this bum. Jeff Baines.'

Slightly dazed, he wandered out, stood by the bicycle and again eyed the paper. Bum it said. He could think of several on the ship who would have exploded with wrath over that. His attention drifted to the second shop farther along. It had a window crammed with comestibles and two big words on the sign-strip above: *Seth's Gulpher.*

Coming to a decision which was encouraged by his innards, he went into Seth's still holding the paper as if it were a death warrant. Inside there was a long counter, some steam and a clatter of crockery. He chose a seat at a marble-topped table occupied by a grey-eyed brunette.

'Do you mind?' he inquired politely, as he lowered himself into a chair.

'Mind what?' She examined his ears as if they were curious phenomena. 'Babies, dogs, aged relations or going out in the rain?'

'Do you mind me being here?'

'I can please myself whether or not I endure it. That's freedom, isn't it?'

'Yeah,' said Harrison. 'Sure it is.' He fidgeted in his seat, feeling somehow that he'd made a move and promptly lost a pawn. He sought around for something else to say and at that point a thin-featured man in a white coat dumped before him a plate loaded with fried chicken and three kinds of unfamiliar vegetables.

The sight unnerved him. He couldn't remember how many years it was since he last saw fried chicken, nor how many months since he'd had vegetables in other than powder form.

'Well,' said the waiter, mistaking his fascinated gaze upon

the food. 'Doesn't it suit you?'

'Yes,' Harrison handed over the slip of paper. 'You bet it does.'

Glancing at the note, the other called to someone semivisible in the steam at one end of the counter, 'You've killed another of Jeff's.' He went away, tearing the slip into small pieces.

'That was a fast pass,' commented the brunette, nodding at the loaded plate. 'He dumps a feed-ob on you and you bounce it straight back, leaving all quits. I'll have to wash dishes to get rid of mine, or kill one Seth has got on somebody else.'

'I stacked a load of canned stuff.' Harrison picked up knife and fork, his mouth watering. There were no knives and forks on the ship. They weren't needed for powders and pills. 'Don't give you any choice here, do they? You take what you get.'

'Not if you've got an ob on Seth,' she informed. 'In that case, he's got to work it off best way he can. You should have put that to him instead of waiting for fate and complaining afterwards.'

'I'm not complaining.'

'It's your right. That's freedom, isn't it?' She mused a bit, went on, 'Isn't often I'm a plant ahead of Seth, but when I am I scream for iced pineapple and he comes running. When *he's* a plant ahead, *I* do the running.' Her grey eyes narrowed in sudden suspicion, and she added, 'You're listening like it's all new to you. Are you a stranger here?'

He nodded, his mouth full of chicken. A little later he managed, 'I'm off that spaceship.'

'Good grief!' She froze considerably. 'An Antigand! I wouldn't have thought it. Why, you look almost human.'

'I've long taken pride in that similarity,' his wit rising along with his belly. He chewed, swallowed, looked around. The white-coated man came up. 'What's to drink?' Harrison asked.

'Dith, double-dith, shemak or coffee.'

'Coffee. Big and black.'

'Shemak is better,' advised the brunette as the waiter went away. 'But why should I tell you?'

The coffee came in a pint-sized mug. Dumping it, the waiter said, 'It's your choice seeing Seth's working one off. What'll you have for after – apple pie, yimpik delice, grated

55

tarfelsoufers or canimelon in syrup?'

'Iced pineapple.'

'Ugh!' The other blinked at Harrison, gave the brunette an accusing stare, went away and got it.

Harrison pushed it across. 'Take the plunge and enjoy yourself.'

'It's yours.'

'Couldn't eat it if I tried.' He dug up another load of chicken, stirred his coffee, began to feel at peace with the world. 'Got as much as I can manage right here.' He made an inviting motion with his fork. 'G'wan, be greedy and to heck with the waistline.'

'No.' Firmly she pushed the pineapple back at him. 'If I got through that, I'd be loaded with an ob.'

'So what?'

'I don't let strangers plant obs on me.'

'Quite right, too. Very proper of you,' approved Harrison. 'Strangers often have strange notions.'

'You've been around,' she agreed. 'Only I don't know what's strange about the notions.'

'Dish washer!'

'Eh?'

'Cynic,' he translated. 'One washes dishes in a cynic.' The pineapple got another pass in her direction. 'If you feel I'll be dumping an ob which you'll have to pay off, you can do it in a seemly manner right here. All I want is some information. Just tell me where I can put my finger on the ripest cheese in the locality.'

'That's an easy one. Go round to Alec Peters's place, middle of Tenth Street.' With that, she dug into the dish.

'Thanks, I was beginning to think everyone was dumb or afflicted with the funnies.'

He carried on with his own meal, finished it, lay back expansively. Unaccustomed nourishment got his brain working a bit more dexterously, for after a minute an expression of deep suspicion clouded his face and he inquired, 'Does this Peters run a cheese warehouse?'

'Of course.' Emitting a sigh of pleasure, she put aside her empty dish.

56

He groaned low down, then informed, 'I'm chasing the mayor.'

'What is that?'

'Number one. The big boss. The sheriff, pohanko, or whatever you call him.'

'I'm no wiser,' she said, genuinely puzzled.

'The man who runs this town. The leading citizen.'

'Make it a little clearer,' she suggested, trying hard to help him. 'Who or what should this citizen be leading?'

'You and Seth and everyone else.' He waved a hand to encompass the entire burg.

Frowning, she said, 'Leading us *where*?'

'Wherever you're going.'

She gave up, beaten, and signed the white-coated waiter to come to her assistance.

'Matt, are we going any place?'

'How should I know?'

'Well, ask Seth then.'

He went away, came back with, 'Seth says he's going home at six o'clock and what's it to you?'

'Anyone leading him there?' she inquired.

'Don't be daft,' Matt advised. 'He knows his own way and he's cold sober.'

Harrison chipped in with, 'Look, I don't see why there should be so much difficulty about this. Just tell me where I can find an official, any official! — the police chief, the city treasurer, the mortuary keeper or even a mere justice of the peace.'

'What's an official?' asked Matt, openly puzzled.

'What's a justice of the peace?' added the brunette.

His mind side-slipped and did a couple of spins. It took him quite a while to reassemble his thoughts and try another tack.

'Supposing,' he said to Matt, 'this joint catches fire. What would you do?'

'Fan it to keep it going,' responded Matt, fed up and making no effort to conceal the fact. He returned to the counter with the air of one who has no time to waste on half-wits.

'He'd put it out,' informed the brunette. 'What else would you expect him to do?'

'Supposing he couldn't?'

'He'd call in others to help him.'

'And would they?'

'Of course,' she assured, surveying him with pity. 'They'd be planting a nice crop of strong obs, wouldn't they?'

'Yes, I guess so.' He began to feel stalled, but made a last shot at the problem. 'What if the fire were too big and fast for passers-by to tackle?'

'Seth would summon the fire squad.'

Defeat receded. A touch of triumph replaced it.

'Ah, so there is a fire squad! That's what I meant by something official. That's what I've been after all along. Quick, tell me where I can find the depot.'

'Bottom end of Twelfth. You can't miss it.'

'Thanks.' He got up in a hurry. 'See you again sometime.' Going out fast, he grabbed his bicycle, shoved off from the kerb.

The fire depot was a big place holding four telescopic ladders, a spray tower and two multiple pumps, all motorized on the usual array of fat rubber balls. Inside, Harrison came face to face with a small man wearing immense plus fours.

'Looking for someone?' asked the small man.

'The fire chief,' said Harrison.

'Who's he?'

By this time prepared for that sort of thing, Harrison spoke as one would to a child. 'See here, mister, this is a fire-fighting outfit. Somebody bosses it. Somebody organizes the shebang, fills forms, presses buttons, recommends promotions, kicks the shiftless, takes all the credit, transfers all the blame and generally lords it around. He's the most important guy in the bunch and everybody knows it.' His forefinger tapped the other's chest. 'And he's the fella I'm going to talk to if it's the last thing I do.'

'Nobody's any more important than anyone else. How can they be? I think you're crazy.'

'You're welcome to think what you like, but I'm telling you that – '

A shrill bell clamoured, cutting off the sentence. Twenty men appeared as if by magic, boarded a ladder and a multipump, roared into the street.

Squat, basin-shaped helmets were the crew's only item of common attire. Apart from these, they plumbed the depths of sartorial iniquity. The man with the plus fours, who had gained the pump in one bold leap, was whirled out standing between a fat fire-fighter wearing a rainbow-hued cummerbund and a thin one sporting a canary yellow kilt. A latecomer decorated with earrings shaped like little bells hotly pursued the pump, snatched at its tailboard, missed, disconsolately watched the outfit disappear from sight. He mooched back, swinging his helmet in one hand.

'Just my lousy luck,' he informed the gaping Harrison. 'The sweetest call of the year. A big brewery. The sooner they get there the bigger the obs they'll plant on it.' He licked his lips at the thought, sat on a coil of canvas hose. 'Oh, well, maybe it's all for the good of my health.'

'Tell me something,' Harrison insisted. 'How do you get a living?'

'There's a heck of a question. You can see for yourself. I'm on the fire squad.'

'I know. What I mean is, who pays you?'

'Pays me?'

'Gives you money for all this.'

'You talk kind of peculiar. What is money?'

Harrison rubbed his cranium to assist the circulation of blood through the brain. What is money? Yeouw. He tried another angle.

'Supposing your wife needs a new coat, how does she get it?'

'Goes to a store saddled with fire-obs, of course. She kills one or two for them.'

'But what if no clothing store has had a fire?'

'You're pretty ignorant, brother. Where in this world do you come from?' His ear bells swung as he studied the other a moment, then went on. 'Almost all stores have fire-obs. If they've any sense, they allocate so many per month by way of insurance. They look ahead, just in case, see? They plant obs on us, in a way, so that when we rush to the rescue we've got to kill off a dollop of theirs before we can plant any new ones of our own. That stops us overdoing it and making hogs of ourselves. Sort of cuts down the stores' liabilities. It makes sense, doesn't it?'

'Maybe, but – '

'I get it now,' interrupted the other, narrowing his eyes. 'You're from that spaceship. You're an Antigand.'

'I'm a Terran,' said Harrison with suitable dignity. 'What's more, all the folk who originally settled this planet were Terrans.'

'You trying to teach me history?' He gave a harsh laugh. 'You're wrong. There was a five per cent strain of Martian.'

'Even the Martians are descended from Terran settlers,' riposted Harrison.

'So what? That was a devil of a long time back. Things change, in case you haven't heard. We've no Terrans or Martians on this world – except for your crowd which has come in unasked. We're all Gands here. And you nosey pokes are Antigands.'

'We aren't anti-anything that I know of. Where did you get that idea?'

'Myob!' said the other, suddenly determined to refuse further agreement. He tossed his helmet to one side, spat on the floor.

'Huh?'

'You heard me. Go trundle your scooter.'

Harrison gave up and did just that. He pedalled gloomily back to the ship.

His Excellency pinned him with an authoritative optic. 'So you're back at last, mister. How many are coming and at what time?'

'None, sir,' said Harrison, feeling kind of feeble.

'None?' August eyebrows rose up. 'Do you mean that they have refused my invitation?'

'No, sir.'

The ambassador waited a moment, then said, 'Come out with it, mister. Don't stand there gawking as if your push-and-puff contraption has just given birth to a roller skate. You say they haven't refused my invitation – but nobody is coming. What am I to make of that?'

'I didn't ask anyone.'

'So you didn't ask!' Turning, he said to Grayder, Shelton and the others, 'He didn't ask!' His attention came back to Harrison. 'You forgot all about it, I presume? Intoxicated by liberty and the power of man over machine, you flashed around the town at nothing less than eighteen miles per hour, creating consternation among the citizenry, tossing their traffic laws into the ash can, putting persons in peril of their lives, not even troubling to ring your bell or –'

'I haven't got a bell, sir,' denied Harrison, inwardly resenting this list of enormities. 'I have a whistle operated by rotation of the rear wheel.'

'There!' said the ambassador, like one abandoning all hope. He sat down, smacked his forehead several times. 'Somebody's going to get a bubble-pipe.' He pointed a tragic finger. 'And *he*'s got a whitsle.'

'I designed it myself, sir,' Harrison told him, very informatively.

'I'm sure you did. I can imagine it. I would expect it of you.' The ambassador got a fresh grip on himself. 'Look, mister, tell me something in strict confidence, just between you and me.' He leaned forward, put the question in a whisper that ricocheted seven times around the room. '*Why* didn't you ask anyone?'

'Couldn't find anyone to ask, sir. I did my level best but they didn't seem to know what I was talking about. Or they pretended they didn't.'

'Humph!' His Excellency glanced out of the nearest port, consulted his wrist watch. 'The light is fading already. Night will be upon us pretty soon. It's getting too late for further action.' An annoyed grunt. 'Another day gone to pot. Two days here and we're still fiddling around.' His eye was jaundiced as it rested on Harrison. 'All right, mister, we're wasting time anyway so we might as well hear your story in full. Tell us what happened in complete detail. That way, we may be able to dig some sense out of it.'

Harrison told it, finishing, 'It seemed to me, sir, that I could go on for weeks trying to argue it out with people whose brains are oriented east-west while mine points north-south. You can talk with them from now to doomsday, even get real friendly and enjoy the conversation – without either side knowing what the other is jawing about.'

'So it seems,' commented the ambassador, dryly. He turned to Captain Grayder. 'You've been around a lot and seen many new worlds in your time. What do you make of all this twaddle, if anything?'

'A problem in semantics,' said Grayder, who had been compelled by circumstances to study that subject. 'One comes across it on almost every world that has been long out of touch, though usually it has not developed far enough to get really tough.' He paused reminiscently. 'First guy we met on Basileus said, cordially and in what he fondly imagined was perfect English, "Joy you unboot now!" '

'Yeah? What did that mean?'

'Come inside, put on your slippers and be happy. In other words, welcome! It wasn't difficult to get, your excellency, especially when you expect that sort of thing.' Grayder cast a thoughtful glance at Harrison, went on, 'Here, things appear to have developed to a greater extreme. The language remains fluent, retains enough surface similarities to conceal deeper changes, but meanings have been altered, concepts discarded, new ones substituted, thought-forms re-angled – and, of course, there is the inevitable impact of locally developed slang.'

'Such as " myob",' offered His Excellency. 'Now there's a queer word without recognizable Earth root. I don't like the way they use it. Sounds downright insulting. Obviously it has some sort of connection with these obs they keep batting around. It means "my obligation" or something like that, but the significance beats me.'

'There is no connection, sir,' Harrison contradicted. He hesitated, saw they were waiting for him, plunged boldly on. 'Coming back I met the lady who directed me to Baines's place. She asked whether I'd found him and I said yes, thank you. We chatted a bit. I asked her what "myob" meant. She said it was initial-slang.' He stopped at that point.

'Keep going,' advised the ambassador. 'After some of the sulphurous comments I've heard coming out of the Blieder-room ventilation-shaft, I can stomach anything. What does it mean?'

62

'M-y-o-b,' informed Harrison, blinking. 'Mind your own business.'

'So!' His Excellency gained colour. 'So that's what they've been telling me all along?'

'I'm afraid so, sir.'

'Evidently they've a lot to learn.' His neck swelled with sudden undiplomatic fury, he smacked a large hand on the table and said, loudly, 'And they are going to learn it!'

'Yes, sir,' agreed Harrison, becoming more uneasy and wanting out. 'May I go now and attend to my bicycle?'

'Get out of my sight!' shouted the ambassador. He made a couple of meaningless gestures, turned a florid face on Captain Grayder. 'Bicycle! Does anyone on this vessel own a slingshot?'

'I doubt it, your excellency, but I will make inquiries, if you wish.'

'Don't be an imbecile,' ordered His Excellency. 'We have our full quota of hollow-heads already.'

Postponed until early morning, the next conference was relatively short and sweet. His Excellency took a seat, har-umphed, straightened his best, frowned around the table.

'Let's have another look at what we've got. We know that this planet's mules call themselves Gands, don't take much interest in their Terran origin and insist on referring to us as Antigands. That implies an education and resultant outlook inimical to ourselves. They've been trained from childhood to take it for granted that whenever we appeared upon the scene we would prove to be against whatever they are for.'

'And we haven't the remotest notion of what they're for,' put in Colonel Shelton, quite unnecessarily. But it served to show that he was among those present and paying attention.

'I am grimly aware of our ignorance in that respect,' endorsed the ambassador. 'They are maintaining a conspiracy of silence about their prime motivation. We've got to break it somehow.' He cleared his throat, continued, 'They have a peculiar nonmonetary economic system which, in my opinion, manages to function only because of large surpluses. It won't stand a day when overpopulation brings serious shortages. This economic setup appears to be based on co-operative techniques, private enterprise, a kindergarten's honour system and plain unadorned gimme. That makes it a good deal crazier than that food-in-the-bank wackidoo they've got on the four outer planets of the Epsilon system.'

'But it works,' observed Grayder, pointedly.

'After a fashion. That flap-eared engineer's bicycle works – and so does he! A motorized job would save him a lot of sweat.' Pleased with this analogy, the ambassador mused over it a few seconds. 'This local scheme of economics – if you can call it a scheme – almost certainly is the end result of the haphazard development of some hick eccentricity brought in by the original settlers. It is overdue for motorizing, so to speak. They know it but don't want it because mentally they're three hundred years behind the times. They're afraid of change, improvement, efficiency – like most backward peoples. Moreover, some of them have a vested interest in keeping things as they are.' He sniffed loudly to express his contempt. 'They are antagonistic towards us simply because they don't want to be disturbed.'

His authoritative stare went round the table, daring one of them to remark that this might be as good a reason as any. They were too disciplined to fall into that trap. None offered comment, so he went on.

'In due time, after we've got a grip on affairs, we are going to have a long and tedious task on our hands. We'll have to overhaul their entire educational system with a view to eliminating anti-Terran prejudices and bringing them up to date on the facts of life. We've had to do that on several other planets, though not to anything like the same extent as will be necessary here.'

'We'll cope,' promised someone.

Ignoring him, the ambassador finished, 'However, all of that is in the future. We've a problem to solve in the present. It's in our laps right now, namely, where are the reins of power and who's holding them? We've got to solve that before we can make progress. How're we going to do it?' He leaned back in his chair, added, 'Get your wits working and let me have some bright suggestions.'

Captain Grayder stood up, a big, leather-bound book in his

hands. 'Your excellency, I don't think we need exercise our minds over new plans for making contact and gaining essential information. It looks as if the next move is going to be imposed upon us.'

'How do you mean?'

'There are a good many old-timers in my crew. Space lawyers, every one of them.' He tapped the book. 'They know official Space Regulations as well as I do. Sometimes I think they know too much.'

'And so – ?'

Grayder opened the book. 'Regulation 127 says that on a hostile world a crew serves on a war-footing until back in space. On a nonhostile world, they serve on a peace-footing.'

'What of it?'

'Regulation 131A says that on a peace-footing, the crew – with the exception of a minimum number required to keep the vessel's essential services in trim – is entitled to land-leave immediately after unloading of cargo or within seventy-two Earth hours of arrival, whichever period is the shorter.' He glanced up. 'By midday the men will be all set for land-leave and itching to go. There will be ructions if they don't get it.'

'Will there now?' said the ambassador, smiling lopsidedly. 'What if I say this world is hostile? That'll pin their ears back, won't it?'

Impassively consulting his book, Grayder came back with, 'Regulation 148 says that a hostile world is defined as any planet that systematically opposes Empire citizens by force.' He turned the next page. 'For the purpose of these regulations, force is defined as any course of action calculated to inflict physical injury, whether or not said action succeeds in its intent.'

'I don't agree.' The ambassador registered a deep frown. 'A world can be psychologically hostile without resorting to force. We've an example right here. It isn't a friendly world.'

'There are no friendly worlds within the meaning of Space Regulations,' Grayder informed. 'Every planet falls into one of two classifications: hostile or nonhostile.' He tapped the hard leather cover. 'It's all in the book.'

'We would be prize fools to let a mere book boss us around or allow the crew to boss us, either. Throw it out of the port.

Stick it into the disintegrator. Get rid of it any way you like – and forget it.'

'Begging your pardon, your excellency, but I can't do that.' Grayder opened the tome at the beginning. 'Basic regulations 1A, 1B and 1C include the following: whether in space or on land, a vessel's personnel remain under direct command of its captain or his nominee who will be guided entirely by Space Regulations and will be responsible only to the Space Committee situated upon Terra. The same applies to all troops, officials and civilian passengers aboard a space-traversing vessel, whether in flight or grounded – regardless of rank or authority they are subordinate to the captain or his nominee. A nominee is defined as a ship's officer performing the duties of an immediate superior when the latter is incapacitated or absent.'

'All that means you are king of your castle,' said the ambassador, none too pleased. 'If we don't like it, we must get off the ship.'

'With the greatest respect to yourself, I must agree that that is the position. I cannot help it – regulations are regulations. And the men know it!' Grayder dumped the book, poked it away from him. 'Ten to one the men will wait to midday, pressing their pants, creaming their hair and so forth. They will then make approach to me in proper manner to which I cannot object. They will request the first mate to submit their leave-roster for my approval.' He gave a deep sigh. 'The worst I could do would be to quibble about certain names on the roster and switch a few men around – but I couldn't refuse leave to a full quota.'

'Liberty to paint the town red might be a good thing after all,' suggested Colonel Shelton, not averse to doing some painting himself. 'A dump like this wakes up when the fleet's in port. We ought to get contacts by the dozens. That's what we want, isn't it?'

'We want to pin down this planet's leaders,' the ambassador pointed out. 'I can't see them powdering their faces, putting on their best hats and rushing out to invite the yoohoo from a bunch of hungry sailors.' His plump features quirked. 'We have got to find the needles in this haystack. That job won't be done by a gang of ratings on the rampage.'

Grayder put in, 'I'm inclined to agree with you, Your Excellency, but we'll have to take a chance on it. If the men want to go out, the circumstances deprive me of power to prevent them. Only one thing can give me the power.'

'And what is that?'

'Evidence enabling me to define this world as hostile within the meaning of Space Regulations.'

'Well, can't we arrange that somehow?' Without waiting for a reply, the ambassador continued. 'Every crew has its incurable trouble-maker. Find yours, give him a double shot of Venusian cognac, tell him he's being granted immediate leave – but you doubt whether he'll enjoy it because these Gands view us as reasons why people dig up the drains. Then push him out of the lock. When he comes back with a black eye and a boastful story about the other fellow's condition, declare this world hostile.' He waved an expressive hand. 'And there you are. Physical violence. All according to the book.'

'Regulation 148A, emphasizing that opposition by force must be systematic, warns that individual brawls may not be construed as evidence of hostility.'

The ambassador turned an irate face upon the senior civil servant: 'When you get back to Terra – if ever you do get back – you can tell the appropriate department how the space service is balled up, hamstrung, semiparalysed and generally handicapped by bureaucrats who write books.'

Before the other could think up a reply complimentary to his kind without contradicting the ambassador, a knock came at the door. First Mate Morgan entered, saluted smartly, offered Captain Grayder a sheet of paper.

'First liberty roll, sir. Do you approve it?'

Four hundred and twenty men hit the town in the early afternoon. They advanced upon it in the usual manner of men overdue for the bright lights, that is to say, eagerly, expectantly, in buddy-bunches of two, three, six or ten.

Gleed attached himself to Harrison. They were two odd rankers, Gleed being the only sergeant on leave, Harrison the only tenth engineer. They were also the only two fish out of water since both were in civilian clothes and Gleed missed his uniform while Harrison felt naked without his bicycle. These trifling features gave them enough in common to justify at least one day's companionship.

'This one's a honey,' declared Gleed with immense enthusiasm. 'I've been on a good many liberty jaunts in my time but this one's a honey. On all other trips the boys ran up against the same problem – what to use for money. They had to go forth like a battalion of Santa Clauses, loaded up with anything that might serve for barter. Almost always ninetenths of it wasn't of any use and had to be carted back again.'

'On Persephone,' informed Harrison, 'a long-shanked Milik offered me a twenty-carat, blue-tinted first-water diamond for my bike.'

'Jeepers, didn't you take it?'

'What was the good? I'd have had to go back sixteen lightyears for another one.'

'You could do without a bike for a bit.'

'I can do without a diamond. I can't ride around on a diamond.'

'Neither can you sell a bicycle for the price of a sportster Moonboat.'

'Yes I can. I just told you this Milik offered me a rock like an egg.'

'It's a crying shame. You'd have got two hundred to two fifty thousand credits for that blinder, if it was flawless.' Sergeant Gleed smacked his lips at the thought of so much moola stacked on the head of a barrel. 'Credits and plenty of them – that's what I love. And that's what makes this trip a honey. Every other time we've gone out, Grayder has first lectured us about creating a favourable impression, behaving in a spacemanlike manner, and so forth. This time, he talks about credits.'

'The ambassador put him up to that.'

'I liked it, all the same,' said Gleed. 'Ten credits, a bottle of cognac and double liberty for every man who brings back to the ship an adult Gand, male or female, who is sociable and willing to talk.'

'It won't be easily earned.'

'One hundred credits to whoever gets the name and address of the town's chief civic dignity. A thousand credits for the name and accurate location of the world's capital city.' He whistled happily, added, 'Somebody's going to be in the dough and it won't be Bidworthy. He didn't come out of the hat, I know – I was holding it.'

He ceased talking, turned to watch a tall, lithe blonde striding past. Harrison pulled at his arm.

'Here's Baines's place that I told you about. Let's go in.'

'Oh, all right.' Gleed followed with much reluctance, his gaze still down the street.

'Good afternoon,' said Harrison, brightly.

'It ain't,' contradicted Jeff Baines. 'Trade's bad. There's a semifinal being played and it's taken half the town away. They'll think about their bellies after I've closed. Probably make a rush on me tomorrow and I won't be able to serve them fast enough.'

'How can trade be bad if you don't take money even when it's good?' inquired Gleed, reasonably applying what information Harrison had given him.

Jeff's big moon eyes went over him slowly, then turned to Harrison. 'So he's another bum off your boat. What's he talking about?'

'Money,' said Harrison. 'It's stuff we use to simplify trade. It's printed stuff, like documentary obs of various sizes.'

'That tells me a lot,' Jeff Baines observed. 'It tells me a crowd that has to make a printed record of every ob isn't to be trusted – because they don't even trust each other.' Waddling to his high stool, he squatted on it. His breathing was laboured and wheezy. 'And that confirms what our schools have always taught – that an Antigand would swindle his widowed mother.'

'Your schools have got it wrong,' assured Harrison.

'Maybe they have.' Jeff saw no need to argue the point. 'But we'll play safe until we know different.' He looked them over. 'What do you two want, anyway?'

'Some advice,' shoved in Gleed, quickly. 'We're out on the spree. Where's the best places to go for food and fun?'

'How long you got?'

'Until nightfall tomorrow.'

'No use.' Jeff Baines shook his head sorrowfully. 'It'd take

69

you from now to then to plant enough obs to qualify for what's going. Besides, lots of folk wouldn't let any Antigand dump an ob on them. They're kind of particular, see?'

'Look,' said Harrison. 'Can't we get so much as a square meal?'

'Well, I dunno about that.' Jeff thought it over, rubbing several chins. 'You might manage so much – but I can't help you this time. There's nothing I want of you, so you can't use any obs I've got planted.'

'Can you make any suggestions?'

'If you were local citizens, it'd be different. You could get all you want right now by taking on a load of obs to be killed sometime in the future as and when the chances come along. But I can't see anyone giving credit to Antigands who are here today and gone tomorrow.'

'Not so much of the gone tomorrow talk,' advised Gleed. 'When an Imperial Ambassador is sent it means that Terrans will be here for keeps.'

'Who says so?'

'The Empire says so. You're part of it, aren't you?'

'Nope,' said Jeff. 'We aren't part of anything and don't want to be, either. What's more, nobody's going to make us part of anything.'

Gleed leaned on the counter and gazed absently at a large can of pork. 'Seeing I'm out of uniform and not on parade, I sympathize with you though I still shouldn't say it. I wouldn't care to be taken over body and soul by other-world bureaucrats, myself. But you folk are going to have a tough time beating us off. That's the way it is.'

'Not with what we've got,' Jeff opined. He seemed mighty self-confident.

'You ain't got so much,' scoffed Gleed, more in friendly criticism than open contempt. He turned to Harrison. 'Have they?'

'It wouldn't appear so,' ventured Harrison.

'Don't go by appearances,' Jeff advised. 'We've more than you'd care to guess at.'

'Such as what?'

'Well, just for a start, we've got the mightiest weapon ever thought up by mind of man. We're Gands, see? So we don't need ships and guns and suchlike playthings. We've got something better. It's effective. There's no defence against it.'

'I'd like to see it,' Gleed challenged. Data on a new and exceptionally powerful weapon should be a good deal more valuable than the mayor's address. Grayder might be sufficiently overcome by the importance thereof to increase the take to five thousand credits. With a touch of sarcasm, he added, 'But, of course, I can't expect you to give away secrets.'

'There's nothing secret about it,' said Jeff, very surprisingly. 'You can have it for free any time you want. Any Gand would give it you for the asking. Like to know why?'

'You bet.'

'Because it works one way only. We can use it against you – but you can't use it against us.'

'There's no such thing. There's no weapon inventable which the other guy can't employ once he gets his hands on it and knows how to operate it.'

'You sure?'

'Positive,' said Gleed, with no hesitation whatever. 'I've been in the space-service troops for twenty years and you can't fiddle around that long without learning all about weapons from string bows to H-bombs. You're trying to kid me – and it won't work. A one-way weapon is impossible.'

'Don't argue with him,' Harrison suggested to Baines. 'He'll never be convinced until he's shown.'

'I can see that.' Jeff Baines's face creased in a slow grin. 'I told you that you could have our wonder-weapon for the asking. Why don't you ask?'

'All right, I'm asking.' Gleed put it without much enthusiasm. A weapon that would be presented on request, without even the necessity of first planting a minor ob, couldn't be so mighty after all. His imaginary five thousand credits shrank to five, thence to none. 'Hand it over and let me try it.'

Swivelling heavily on his stool, Jeff reached to the wall, removed a small, shiny plaque from its hook, passed it across the counter.

'You may keep it,' he informed. 'And much good may it do you.'

Gleed examined it, turning it over and over between his fingers. It was nothing more than an oblong strip of substance resembling ivory. One side was polished and bare. The other bore three letters deeply engraved in bold style:

F – I. W.

Glancing up, his features puzzled, he said, 'Call this a weapon?'

'Certainly.'

'Then I don't get it.' He passed the plaque to Harrison. 'Do you?'

'No.' Harrison had a good look at it, spoke to Baines. 'What does this F – I. W. mean?'

'Initial-slang,' informed Baines. 'Made correct by common usage. It has become a worldwide motto. You'll see it all over the place, if you haven't noticed it already.'

'I have spotted it here and there but attached no importance to it and thought nothing of it. I remember now I've seen it inscribed in several places, including Seth's and the fire depot.'

'It was on the sides of that bus we couldn't empty,' added Gleed. 'Didn't mean anything to me.'

'It means plenty,' said Jeff. '*Freedom – I Won't!*'

'That kills me,' Gleed told him. 'I'm stone dead already. I've dropped in my tracks.' He watched Harrison thoughtfully pocketing the plaque. 'A bit of abracadabra. What a weapon!'

'Ignorance is bliss,' remarked Baines, strangely certain of himself. 'Especially when you don't know that what you're playing with is the safety catch of something that goes bang.'

'All right,' challenged Gleed, taking him up on that. 'Tell us how it works.'

'I won't.' The grin reappeared. Baines seemed highly satisfied about something.

'That's a fat lot of help.' Gleed felt let down, especially over those momentarily hoped-for credits. 'You boast about a one-way weapon, toss across a slip of stuff with three letters on it and then go dumb. Any guy can talk out the back of his neck. How about backing up your talk?'

'I won't,' said Baines, his grin becoming broader than ever. He favoured the onlooking Harrison with a fat, significant wink.

It made something spark vividly inside Harrison's mind. His jaw dropped, he took the plaque from his pocket, stared at it as if seeing it for the first time.

'Give it me back,' requested Baines, watching him.

Replacing it in his pocket, Harrison said very firmly, 'I won't.'

Baines chuckled. 'Some folks catch on quicker than others.'

Resenting that remark, Gleed held his hand out to Harrison. 'Let's have another look at that thing.'

'I won't,' said Harrison, meeting him eye for eye.

'Hey, that's not the way – ' Gleed's protesting voice died out. He stood there a moment, his optics slightly glassy while his brain performed several loops. Then, in hushed tones, he said, 'Good grief!'

'Precisely,' approved Baines. 'Grief, and plenty of it. You were a bit slow on the uptake.'

Overcome by the flood of insubordinate ideas now pouring upon him, Gleed said hoarsely to Harrison, 'Come on, let's get out of here. I gotta think. I gotta think some place quiet.'

There was a tiny park with seats and lawns and flowers and a little fountain around which a small bunch of children were playing. Choosing a place facing a colourful carpet of exotic un-Terran blooms, they sat and brooded a while.

In due course, Gleed commented, 'For one solitary guy it would be martyrdom, but for a whole world – ' His voice drifted off, came back. 'I've been taking this about as far as I can make it go and the results give me the leaping fantods.'

Harrison said nothing.

'F'rinstance,' Gleed continued, 'supposing when I go back to the ship that snorting rhinoceros Bidworthy gives me an order. I give him the frozen wolliker and say, "I won't!" He either drops dead or throws me in the clink.'

'That would do you a lot of good.'

'Wait a bit – I ain't finished. I'm in the clink, but the job still needs doing. So Bidworthy picks on someone else. The victim, being a soulmate of mine, also donates the icy optic and says, "I won't!" In the clink he goes and I've got company. Bidworthy tries again. And again. There's more of us warming

73

the jug. It'll only hold twenty. So they take over the engineers' mess.'

'Leave our mess out of this,' Harrison requested.

'They take the mess,' Gleed insisted, thoroughly determined to penalize the engineers. 'Pretty soon it's crammed to the roof with I-won'ters. Bidworthy's still rakin' 'em in as fast as he can go – if by that time he hasn't burst a dozen blood vessels. So they take over the Blieder dormitories.'

'Why keep picking on my crowd?'

'And pile them with bodies ceiling-high,' Gleed said, getting sadistic pleasure out of the notion. 'Until in the end Bidworthy has to get buckets and brushes and go down on his knees and do his own deck-scrubbing while Grayder, Shelton and the rest act as clink guards. By that time, His Loftiness the ambassador is in the galley busily cooking for you and me, assisted by a disconcerted bunch of yes-ing pen-pushers.' He had another somewhat awed look at the picture and finished, 'Holy smoke!'

A coloured ball rolled his way, he stooped, picked it up and held on to it. Promptly a boy of about seven ran up, eyed him gravely.

'Give me my ball, please.'

'I won't,' said Gleed, his fingers firmly around it.

There was no protest, no anger, no tears. The child merely registered disappointment, turned to go away.

'Here you are, sonny.' He tossed the ball.

'Thanks.' Grabbing it, the other ran off.

Harrison said, 'What if every living being in the Empire, all the way from Prometheus to Kaldor Four, across eighteen hundred light-years of space, gets an income-tax demand, tears it up and says, "I won't!"? What happens then?'

'We'd need a second universe for a pen and a third one to provide the guards.'

'There would be chaos,' Harrison went on. He nodded towards the fountain and the children playing around it. 'But it doesn't look like chaos here. Not to my eyes. So that means they don't overdo this blank refusal business. They apply it judiciously on some mutually recognized basis. What that basis might be beats me completely.'

'Me, too.'

74

An elderly man stopped near them, surveyed them hesitantly, decided to pick on a passing youth.

'Can you tell me where I can find the roller for Martinstown?'

'Other end of Eighth,' informed the youth. 'One every hour. They'll fix your manacles before they start.'

'Manacles?' The oldster raised white eyebrows. 'Whatever for?'

'That route runs past the spaceship. The Antigands may try to drag you out.'

'Oh, yes, of course.' He ambled on, glanced again at Gleed and Harrison, remarked in passing, 'These Antigands – such a nuisance.'

'Definitely,' endorsed Gleed. 'We keep telling them to get out and they keep on saying, "We won't." '

The old gentleman missed a step, recovered, gave him a peculiar look, continued on his way.

'One or two seem to cotton on to our accents,' Harrison remarked. 'Though nobody noticed mine when I was having that feed in Seth's.'

Gleed perked up with sudden interest. 'Where you've had one feed you can get another. C'mon, let's try. What have we got to lose?'

'Our patience,' said Harrison. He stood up. 'We'll pick on Seth. If he won't play, we'll have a try at someone else. And if nobody will play, we'll skin out fast before we starve to death.'

'Which appears to be exactly what they want us to do,' Gleed pointed out. He scowled to himself. 'They'll get their way over my dead body.'

'That's how,' agreed Harrison. 'Over your dead body.'

Matt came up with a cloth over one arm. 'I'm serving no Antigands.'

'You served me last time,' Harrison told him.

'That's as maybe. I didn't know you were off that ship. But I know now!' He flicked the cloth across one corner of the table. 'No Antigands served by me.'

'Is there any other place where we might get a meal?'

'Not unless somebody will let you plant an ob on them.

75

They won't do that if they're wise to you, but there's a chance they might make the same mistake I did.' Another flick across the corner. 'I don't make them twice.'

'You're making another right now,' said Gleed, his voice tough and authoritative. He nudged Harrison. 'Watch this!' His hand came out of a side pocket holding a tiny blaster. Pointing it at Matt's middle, he continued, 'Ordinarily, I could get into trouble for this, if those on the ship were in the mood to make trouble. But they aren't. They're soured up on you two-legged mules.' He motioned the weapon. 'Get walking and bring us two full plates.'

'I won't,' said Matt, firming his jaw and ignoring the gun.

Gleed thumbed the safety catch which moved with an audible click.

'It's touchy now. It'd go off at a sneeze. Start moving.'

'I won't,' insisted Matt.

Gleed disgustedly shoved the weapon back into his pocket. 'I was only kidding you. It isn't energized.'

'Wouldn't have made the slightest difference if it had been,' Matt assured. 'I serve no Antigands, and that's that!'

'Suppose I'd gone haywire and blown you in half?'

'How could I have served you then?' he inquired. 'A dead person is of no use to anyone. Time you Antigands learned a little logic.'

With that parting shot he went away.

'He's got something there,' observed Harrison, patently depressed. 'What can you do with a waxie one? Nothing whatever! You'd have put him clean out of your own power.'

'Don't know so much. A couple of stiffs lying around might sharpen the others. They'd get really eager.'

'You're thinking of them in Terran terms,' Harrison said. 'It's a mistake. They're not Terrans, no matter where they came from originally. They're Gands.' He mused a moment. 'I've no notion of just what Gands are supposed to be but I reckon they're some kind of fanatics. Terra exported one-track-minders by the millions around the time of the Great Explosion. Look at that crazy crowd they've got on Hygeia.'

'I was there once and I tried hard not to look,' confessed Gleed, reminiscently. 'Then I couldn't stop looking. Not so much as a fig leaf between the lot. They insisted that we were obscene because we wore clothes. So eventually we had to take them off. Know what I was wearing at the time we left?'

'A dignified poise,' Harrison suggested.

'That and an identity disc, cupro-silver, official issue, spacemen, for the use of,' Gleed informed. 'Plus three wipes of grease-paint on my left arm to show I was a sergeant. I looked every inch a sergeant – like heck I did!'

'I know. I had a week in that place.'

'We'd a rear admiral on board,' Gleed went on. 'As a fine physical specimen he resembled a pair of badly worn suspenders. He couldn't overawe anyone while in his birthday suit. Those Hygeians cited his deflation as proof that they'd got real democracy, as distinct from our fake version.' He clucked his tongue. 'I'm not so sure they're wrong.'

'The creation of the Empire has created a queer proposition,' Harrison meditated. 'Namely, that Terra is always right while sixteen hundred and forty-two planets are invariably wrong.'

'You're getting kind of seditious, aren't you?'

Harrison said nothing. Gleed glanced at him, found his attention elsewhere, followed his gaze to a brunette who had just entered.

'Nice,' approved Gleed. 'Not too young, not too old. Not too fat, not too thin. Just right.'

'I know her.' Harrison waved to attract her attention.

She tripped lightly across the room, sat at their table. Harrison made the introduction.

'Friend of mine. Sergeant Gleed.'

'Arthur,' corrected Gleed, eyeing her.

'Mine's Elissa,' she told him. 'What's a sergeant supposed to be?'

'A sort of over-above underthing,' Gleed informed. 'I pass along the telling to the guys who do the doing.'

Her eyes widened. 'Do you mean that people really allow themselves to be told?'

'Of course. Why not?'

'It sounds crazy to me.' Her gaze shifted to Harrison. 'I'll be ignorant of *your* name forever, I suppose?'

He hastened to repair the omission, adding, 'But I don't like James. I prefer Jim.'

77

'Then we'll let it be Jim.' She examined the place, looking over the counter, the other tables. 'Has Matt been to you two?'

'Yes. He refuses to serve us.'

She shrugged warm shoulders. 'It's his right. Everyone has the right to refuse. That's freedom, isn't it?'

'We call it mutiny,' said Gleed.

'Don't be so childish,' she reproved. She stood up, moved away. 'You wait here. I'll go see Seth.'

'I don't get this,' admitted Gleed, when she had passed out of earshot. 'According to that fat fella in the delicatessen, their technique is to give us the cold shoulder until we run away in a huff. But this dame acts friendly. She's ... she's –' He stopped while he sought for a suitable word, found it and said, 'She's un-Gandian.'

'Not so,' Harrison contradicted. 'They've the right to say "I won't." She's practising it.'

'By ghost, yes! I hadn't thought of that. They can work it any way they like, and please themselves.'

'Sure.' He dropped his voice. 'Here she comes.'

Resuming her seat, she primped her hair, said, 'Seth will serve us personally.'

'Another traitor,' remarked Gleed with a grin.

'On one condition,' she went on. 'You two must wait and have a talk with him before you leave.'

'Cheap at the price,' Harrison decided. A thought struck him and he asked, 'Does this mean you'll have to kill several obs for all three of us?'

'Only one for myself.'

'How come?'

'Seth's got ideas of his own. He doesn't feel happy about Antigands any more than does anyone else.'

'And so?'

'But he's got the missionary instinct. He doesn't agree entirely with the idea of giving all Antigands the ghost-treatment. He thinks it should be reserved only for those too stubborn or stupid to be converted.' She smiled at Gleed, making his top hairs quiver. 'Seth thinks that any intelligent Antigand is a would-be Gand.'

'What is a Gand, anyway?' asked Harrison.

'An inhabitant of this world, of course.'

78

'I mean, where did they dig up the name?'

'From Gandhi,' she said.

Harrison frowned in puzzlement. 'Who the deuce was he?'

'An ancient Terran. The one who invented The Weapon.'

'Never heard of him.'

'That doesn't surprise me,' she remarked.

'Doesn't it?' He felt a little irritated. 'Let me tell you that these days we Terrans get as good an education as – '

'Calm down, Jim.' She made it more soothing by pronouncing it 'Jeem'. 'All I mean is that ten to one he's been blanked out of your history books. He might have given you unwanted ideas, see? You couldn't be expected to know what you've been deprived of the chance to learn.'

'If you mean that Terran history is censored, I don't believe it,' he asserted.

'It's your right to refuse to believe. That's freedom, isn't it?'

'Up to a point. A man has duties. He's no right to refuse those.'

'No?' She raised tantalizing eyebrows, delicately curved. 'Who defines those duties – himself, or somebody else?'

'His superiors, most times.'

'No man is superior to another. No man has the right to define another man's duties.' She paused, eyeing him speculatively. 'If anyone on Terra exercises such idiotic power, it is only because idiots permit him. They fear freedom. They prefer to be told. They like being ordered around. What men!'

'I shouldn't listen to you,' protested Gleed, chipping in. His leathery face was flushed. 'You're as naughty as you're pretty.'

'Afraid of your own thoughts?' she jibed, pointedly ignoring his compliment.

He went redder. 'Not on your life. But I – ' His voice trailed off as Seth arrived with three loaded plates and dumped them on the table.

'See you afterwards,' reminded Seth. He was medium-sized, with thin features and sharp, quick-moving eyes. 'Got something to say to you.'

Seth joined them shortly after the end of the meal. Taking a chair, he wiped condensed steam off his face, looked them over.

'How much do you two know?'

'Enough to argue about it,' put in Elissa. 'They are bothered about duties, who defines them, and who does them.'

'With good reason,' Harrison riposted. 'You can't escape them yourselves.'

'Meaning – ?' asked Seth.

'This world runs on some strange system of swapping obligations. How will any person kill an ob unless he recognizes his duty to do so?'

'Duty has nothing to do with it,' said Seth. 'And if it did happen to be a matter of duty, every man would recognize it for himself. It would be outrageous impertinence for anyone else to remind him, unthinkable to anyone to order him.'

'Some guys must make an easy living,' interjected Gleed. 'There's nothing to stop them that I can see.' He studied Seth briefly before he continued, 'How can you cope with a citizen who has no conscience?'

'Easy as pie.'

Elissa suggested, 'Tell them the story of Idle Jack.'

'It's a kid's yarn,' explained Seth. 'All children here know it by heart. It's a classic fable like . . . like – ' He screwed up his face. 'I've lost track of the Terran tales the first comers brought with them.'

'Red Riding Hood,' offered Harrison.

'Yes.' Seth seized on it gratefully. 'Something like that one. A nursery story.' He licked his lips, began, 'This Idle Jack came from Terra as a baby, grew up in our new world, studied our economic system and thought he'd be mighty smart. He decided to become a scratcher.'

'What's a scratcher?' inquired Gleed.

'One who lives by taking obs and does nothing about killing them or planting any of his own. One who accepts everything that's going and gives nothing in return.'

'I get it. I've known one or two like that in my time.'

'Up to age sixteen, Jack got away with it. He was a kid, see. All kids tend to scratch to a certain extent. We expect it and allow for it. After sixteen, he was soon in the soup.'

'How?' urged Harrison, more interested than he was willing to show.

'He went around the town gathering obs by the armful.

80

Meals, clothes and all sorts for the mere asking. It's not a big town. There are no big ones on this planet. They're just small enough for everyone to know everyone – and everyone does plenty of gabbing. Within three or four months the entire town knew Jack was a determined scratcher.'

'Go on,' said Harrison, getting impatient.

'Everything dried up,' said Seth. 'Wherever Jack went, people gave him the "I won't". That's freedom, isn't it? He got no meals, no clothes, no entertainment, no company, nothing! Soon he became terribly hungry, busted into someone's larder one night, gave himself the first square meal in a week.'

'What did they do about that?'

'Nothing. Not a thing.'

'That would encourage him some, wouldn't it?'

'How could it?' Seth asked, with a thin smile. 'It did him no good. Next day his belly was empty again. He had to repeat the performance. And the next day. And the next. People became leery, locked up their stuff, kept watch on it. It became harder and harder. It became so unbearably hard that it was soon a lot easier to leave the town and try another. So Idle Jack went away.'

'To do the same again,' Harrison suggested.

'With the same results for the same reasons,' retorted Seth. 'On he went to a third town, a fourth, a fifth, a twentieth. He was stubborn enough to be witless.'

'He was getting by,' Harrison observed. 'Taking all at the mere cost of moving around.'

'No he wasn't. Our towns are small, like I said. And folk do plenty of visiting from one to another. In town number two Jack had to risk being seen and talked about by someone from town number one. As he went on it got a whole lot worse. In the twentieth he had to take a chance on gabby visitors from any of the previous nineteen.' Seth leaned forward, said with emphasis, 'He never got to town number twenty-eight.'

'No?'

'He lasted two weeks in number twenty-five, eight days in twenty-six, one day in twenty-seven. That was almost the end.'

'What did he do then?'

81

'Took to the open country, tried to live on roots and wild berries. Then he disappeared – until one day some walkers found him swinging from a tree. The body was emaciated and clad in rags. Loneliness and self-neglect had killed him. That was Idle Jack, the scratcher. He wasn't twenty years old.'

'On Terra,' informed Gleed, 'we don't hang people merely for being lazy.'

'Neither do we,' said Seth. 'We leave them free to go hang themselves.' He eyed them shrewdly, went on, 'But don't let it worry you. Nobody has been driven to such drastic measures in my lifetime, leastways, not that I've heard about. People honour their obs as a matter of economic necessity and not from any sense of duty. Nobody gives orders, nobody pushes anyone around, but there's a kind of compulsion built into the circumstances of this planet's way of living. People play square – or they suffer. Nobody enjoys suffering – not even a numbskull.'

'Yes, I suppose you're right,' put in Harrison, much exercised in mind.

'You bet I'm dead right!' Seth assured. 'But what I wanted to talk to you two about is something more important. It's this: What's your real ambition in life?'

Without hesitation, Gleed said, 'To ride the spaceways while remaining in one piece.'

'Same here,' Harrison contributed.

'I guessed that much. You'd not be in the space service if it wasn't your choice. But you can't remain in it forever. All good things come to an end. What then?'

Harrison fidgeted uneasily. 'I don't care to think of it.'

'Some day, you'll have to,' Seth pointed out. 'How much longer have you got?'

'Four and a half Earth years.'

Seth's gaze turned to Gleed.

'Three Earth years.'

'Not long,' Seth commented. 'I didn't expect you would have much time left. It's a safe bet that any ship penetrating this deeply into space has a crew composed mostly of old-timers getting near the end of their terms. The practised hands get picked for the awkward jobs. By the day your boat lands again on Terra it will be the end of the trail for many of them, won't it?'

'It will for me,' Gleed admitted, none too happy at the thought.

'Time – the older you get the faster it goes. Yet when you leave the service you'll still be comparatively young.' He registered a faint, taunting smile. 'I suppose you'll then obtain a private space vessel and continue roaming the cosmos on your own?'

'Impossible,' declared Gleed. 'The best a rich man can afford is a Moonboat. Puttering to and fro between a satellite and its primary is no fun when you're used to Blieder-zips across the galaxy. The smallest space-going craft is far beyond reach of the wealthiest. Only governments can afford them.'

'By "governments" you mean communities?'

'In a way.'

'Well, then, what are you going to do when your space-roving days are over?'

'I'm not like Big Ears here.' Gleed jerked an indicative thumb at Harrison. 'I'm a trooper and not a technician. So my choice is limited by lack of qualifications.' He rubbed his chin, looked wistful. 'I was born and brought up on a farm. I still know a good deal about farming. So I'd like to get a small one of my own and settle down.'

'Think you'll manage it?' asked Seth, watching him.

'On Falder or Hygeia or Norton's Pink Heaven or some other undeveloped planet. But not on Terra. My savings won't extend to that. I don't get half enough to meet Earth costs.'

'Meaning you can't pile up enough obs?'

'I can't,' agreed Gleed, lugubriously. 'Not even if I saved until I'd got a white beard four feet long.'

'So there's Terra's reward for a long spell of faithful service – forego your heart's desire or get out?'

'Shut up!'

'I won't,' said Seth. He leaned nearer. 'Why do you two think two hundred thousand Gands came to this world, Doukhobors to Hygeia, Quakers to Centauri B., and all the others to their selected haunts? Because Terra's reward for

83

good citizenship was the peremptory order to knuckle down or get out. So we got out.'

'It was just as well, anyway,' Elissa interjected. 'According to our history books, Terra was badly overcrowded. We went away and relieved the pressure.'

'That's beside the point,' reproved Seth. He continued with Gleed. 'You want a farm. It can't be on Terra much as you'd like it there. Terra says, "No! Get out!" So it's got to be some place else.' He waited for that to sink in, then, 'Here, you can have one for the mere taking.' He snapped his fingers. 'Like that!'

'You can't kid me,' said Gleed, wearing the expression of one eager to be kidded. 'Where are the hidden strings?'

'On this planet, any plot of ground belongs to the person in possession, the one who is making use of it. Nobody disputes his claim so long as he continues to use it. All you need do is look around for a suitable piece of unused territory – of which there is plenty – and start using it. From that moment it's yours. Immediately you cease using it and walk out, it's anyone else's, for the taking.'

'Zipping meteors!' Gleed was incredulous.

'Moreover, if you look around long enough and strike really lucky,' Seth continued, 'you might stake first claim to a farm someone else has abandoned because of death, illness, a desire to move elsewhere, a chance at something else he liked better, or any other excellent reason. In that case, you would walk into ground already part-prepared, with farmhouse, milking shed, barns and the rest. And it would be yours, all yours.'

'What would I owe the previous occupant?' asked Gleed.

'Nothing. Not an ob. Why should you? If he isn't buried, he has got out for the sake of something else equally free. He can't have the benefit both ways, coming and going.'

'It doesn't make sense to me. Somewhere there's a snag. Somewhere I've got to pour out hard cash or pile up obs.'

'Of course you do. You start a farm. A handful of local folks help you build a house. They dump heavy obs on you. The carpenter wants farm produce for his family for the next couple of years. You give it, thus killing that ob. You continue giving it for a couple of extra years, thus planting an ob on *him*.

First time you want fences mending, or some other suitable task doing, along he comes to kill *that* ob. And so with all the rest including the people who supply your raw materials, your seeds and machinery, or do your trucking for you.'

'They won't all want milk and potatoes,' Gleed pointed out.

'Don't know what you mean by potatoes. Never heard of them.'

'How can I square up with someone who may be getting all the farm produce he wants from elsewhere ?'

'Easy,' said Seth. 'A tinsmith supplies you with several churns. He doesn't want food. He's getting all he needs from another source. His wife and three daughters are overweight and dieting. The mere thought of a load from your farm gives them the horrors.'

'Well ?'

'But this tinsmith's tailor, or his cobbler, have got obs on him which he hasn't had the chance to kill. So he transfers them to you. As soon as you're able, you give the tailor or cobbler what they need to satisfy the obs, thus doing the tinsmith's killing along with your own.' He gave his usual half-smile, added, 'And everyone is happy.'

Gleed stewed it over, frowning while he did it. 'You're tempting me. You shouldn't ought to. It's a criminal offence to try to divert a spaceman from his allegiance. It's sedition. Terra is tough with sedition.'

'Tough my eye!' said Seth, sniffing contemptuously. 'We've Gand laws here.'

'All you have to do,' suggested Elissa, sweetly persuasive, 'is say to yourself that you've got to go back to the ship, that it's your duty to go back, that neither the ship nor Terra can get along without you.' She tucked a curl away. 'Then be a free individual and say, "I won't!"'

'They'd skin me alive. Bidworthy would preside over the operation in person.'

'I don't think so,' Seth offered. 'This Bidworthy – whom I presume to be anything but a jovial character – stands with you and the rest of your crew at the same junction. The road before him splits two ways. He's got to take one or the other and there's no third alternative. Sooner or later he'll be hell-bent for home, eating his top lip as he goes, or else he'll be running around in a truck delivering your milk – because, deep inside himself, that's what he's always wanted to do.'

'You don't know him like I do,' mourned Gleed. 'He uses a lump of old iron for a soul.'

'Funny,' remarked Harrison, 'I always thought of you that way – until today.'

'I'm off duty,' said Gleed, as though that explained everything. 'I can relax and let the ego zoom around outside of business hours.' He stood up, firmed his jaw. 'But I'm going back on duty. Right now!'

'You're not due before sundown tomorrow,' Harrison protested.

'Maybe I'm not. But I'm going back all the same.'

Elissa opened her mouth, closed it as Seth nudged her. They sat in silence and watched Gleed march determinedly out.

'It's a good sign,' commented Seth, strangely self-assured. 'He's been handed a wallop right where he's weakest.' He chuckled low down, turned to Harrison. 'What's *your* ultimate ambition?'

'Thanks for the meal. It was a good one and I needed it.' Harrison stood up, manifestly embarrassed. He gestured towards the door. 'I'm going to catch him up. If he's returning to the ship, I think I'll do likewise.'

Again Seth nudged Elissa. They said nothing as Harrison made his way out, carefully closing the door behind him.

'Sheep,' decided Elissa, disappointed for no obvious reason. 'One follows another. Just like sheep.'

'Not so,' Seth contradicted. 'They're humans animated by the same thoughts, the same emotions, as were our forefathers who had nothing sheeplike about them.' Twisting round in his chair, he beckoned to Matt. 'Bring us two shemaks.' Then to Elissa. 'My guess is that it won't pay that ship to hang around too long.'

The battleship's caller-system bawled imperatively, 'Fanshaw, Folsom, Fuller, Garson, Gleed, Gregory, Haines, Harrison, Hope – 'and down through the alphabet.

A trickle of men flowed along the passages, catwalks and

alleyways towards the fore chartroom. They gathered outside it in small clusters, chattering in undertones and sending odd scraps of conversation echoing down the corridor.

'Wouldn't say anything to us but, "Myob!" Got sick and tired of it after a while.'

'You ought to have split up, like we did. That show place on the outskirts didn't know what a Terran looks like. I just walked in and took a seat.'

'Hear about Meakin? He mended a leaky roof, chose a bottle of double dith in payment and mopped the lot. He was dead flat when we found him. Had to be carried back.'

'Some guys have all the luck. We got the brush-off wherever we showed our faces. It gets you down.'

'You should have separated, like I said.'

'Half the mess must be still lying in the gutter. They haven't turned up yet.'

'Grayder will be hopping mad. He'd have stopped this morning's second quota if he'd known in time.'

Every now and again First Mate Morgan stuck his head out of the chartroom door and uttered a name already voiced on the caller. Frequently there was no response.

'Harrison!' he yelled.

With a puzzled expression, Harrison went inside. Captain Grayder was there, seated behind a desk and gazing moodily at a list lying before him. Colonel Shelton was stiff and erect to one side, with Major Hame slightly behind him. Both wore the pained expressions of those tolerating a bad smell while the plumber goes looking for the leak.

His Excellency was tramping steadily to and fro in front of the desk, muttering deep down in his chins. 'Barely five days and already the rot has set in.' He turned as Harrison entered, fired off sharply, 'So it's you, mister. When did you return from leave?'

'The evening before last, sir.'

'Ahead of time, eh? That's curious. Did you get a puncture or something?'

'No, sir. I didn't take my bicycle with me.'

'Just as well,' approved the ambassador. 'If you had done so, you'd have been a thousand miles away by now and still pushing hard.'

'Why, sir?'

'Why? He asks me why! That's precisely what I'd like to know – *why?*' He fumed a bit, then inquired, 'Did you visit this town by yourself, or in company?'

'I went with Sergeant Gleed, sir.'

'Call him,' ordered the ambassador, looking at Morgan.

Opening the door, Morgan obediently shouted, 'Gleed! Gleed!'

No answer.

He tried again, without result. They put it over the caller-system again. Sergeant Gleed refused to be among those present.

'Has he booked in?'

Grayder consulted his list. 'In early. Twenty-four hours ahead of time. He may have sneaked out again with the second liberty quota this morning and omitted to book out. That's a double crime.'

'If he's not on the ship, he's off the ship, crime or no crime.'

'Yes, your excellency.' Captain Grayder registered slight weariness.

'GLEED!' howled Morgan, outside the door. A moment later he poked his head inside, said, 'Your excellency, one of the men says Sergeant Gleed is not on board because he saw him in town quite recently.'

'Send him in.' The ambassador made an impatient gesture at Harrison. 'Stay where you are and keep those confounded ears from flapping. I've not finished with you yet.'

A long, gangling grease-monkey came in, blinked around, a little awed by high brass.

'What do you know about Sergeant Gleed?' demanded the ambassador.

The other licked his lips, seemed sorry that he had mentioned the missing man. 'It's like this, your honour, I – '

'Call me "sir".'

'Yes, sir.' More disconcerted blinking. 'I went out with the second party early this morning, came back a couple of hours ago because my stomach was acting up. On the way, I saw Sergeant Gleed and spoke to him.'

'Where? When?'

'In town, sir. He was sitting in one of those big long-distance coaches. I thought it a bit queer.'

'Get down to the roots, man! What did he tell you, if anything?'

'Not much, sir. He seemed pretty chipper about something. Mentioned a young widow struggling to look after two hundred acres. Someone had told him about her and he thought he'd take a peek.' He hesitated, backed away a couple of paces, added, 'He also said I'd see him in irons or never.'

'One of *your* men,' said the ambassador to Colonel Shelton. 'A trooper, allegedly well-disciplined. One with long service, three stripes, and a pension to lose.' His attention returned to the informant. 'Did he say exactly where he was going?'

'No, sir. I asked him, but he just grinned and said, "Myob!" So I came back to the ship.'

'All right. You may go.' His Excellency watched the other depart, then continued with Harrison. 'You were with that first quota.'

'Yes, sir.'

'Let me tell you something, mister. Four hundred and twenty men went out. Only two hundred have returned. Forty of those were in various stages of alcoholic turpitude. Ten of them are in the clink yelling, "I won't!" in steady chorus. Doubtless they'll go on yelling until they've sobered up.'

He stared at Harrison as if that worthy were personally responsible, then went on, 'There's something paradoxical about this. I can understand the drunks. There are always a few individuals who blow their tops first day on land. But of the two hundred who have condescended to come back, about half returned before time, the same as you did. Their reasons were identical – the town was unfriendly, everyone treated them like ghosts until they'd had enough.'

Harrison made no comment.

'So we have two diametrically opposed reactions,' the ambassador complained. 'One gang of men say the place stinks so much that they'd rather be back on the ship. Another gang finds it so hospitable that either they get filled to the gills on some stuff called double dith, or they stay sober and desert the service. I want an explanation. There's got to be one somewhere. You've been twice in this town. What can you tell us?'

Carefully, Harrison said, 'It all depends on whether or not you're spotted as a Terran. Also on whether you meet Gands who'd rather convert you than give you the brush-off.' He pondered a moment, finished, 'Uniforms are a giveaway.'

'You mean they're allergic to uniforms?'

'More or less, sir.'

'Any idea why?'

'Couldn't say for certain, sir. I don't know enough about them yet. At a guess, I think they may have been taught to associate uniforms with the Terran regime from which their ancestors escaped.'

'Escaped nothing!' scoffed the ambassador. 'They grabbed the benefit of Terran inventions, Terran techniques and Terran manufacturing ability to go some place where they'd have more elbow room.' He gave Harrison the sour eye. 'Don't any of them wear uniforms?'

'Not that I could recognize as such. They seem to take pleasure in expressing their individual personalities by wearing anything they fancy, from pigtails to pink boots. Oddity in attire is the norm among the Gands. Uniformity is the real oddity – they think it's submissive and degrading.'

'You refer to them as Gands. Where did they dig up that name?'

Harrison told him, thinking back to Elissa as she explained it. In his mind's eye he could see her now. And Seth's place with the tables set and steam rising behind the counter and mouth-watering smells oozing from the background. Now that he came to visualize the scene again, it appeared to embody an elusive but essential something that the ship had never possessed.

'And this person,' he concluded, 'invented what they call The Weapon.'

'Hm-m-m! And they assert he was a Terran? What does he look like? Did you see a photograph or a statue?'

'They don't erect statues, sir. They say no person is more important than another.'

'Bunkum!' snapped the ambassador, instinctively rejecting that viewpoint. 'Did it occur to you to ask at what period in history this wonderful weapon was tried out?'

'No, sir,' Harrison confessed. 'I didn't think it important.'

'You wouldn't. Some of you men are too slow to catch a Callistrian sloth wandering in its sleep. I don't criticize your abilities as spacemen, but as intelligence-agents you're a dead loss.'

'I'm sorry, sir,' said Harrison.

Sorry? You louse! whispered something deep within his own mind. *Why should you be sorry? He's only a pompous fat man who couldn't kill an ob if he tried. He's no better than you. Those raw boys prancing around on Hygeia would maintain that he's not as good as you because he's got a pot belly. Yet you keep looking at his pot belly and saying, 'Sir', and 'I'm sorry'. If he tried to ride your bike, he'd fall off before he'd gone ten yards. Go spit in his eye and say, 'I won't'. You're not scared, are you?*

'*No!*' announced Harrison, loudly and firmly.

Captain Grayder glanced up. 'If you're going to start answering questions before they've been asked, you'd better see the medic. Or have we a telepath on board?'

'I was thinking,' Harrison explained.

'I approve of that,' put in His Excellency. He lugged a couple of huge tomes out of the wall-shelves, began to thumb rapidly through them. 'Do plenty of thinking whenever you've the chance and it will become a habit. It will get easier and easier as time rolls on. In fact, a day may come when it can be done without pain.'

He shoved the books back, pulled out two more, spoke to Major Hame who happened to be at his elbow. 'Don't pose there glassy-eyed like a relic propped up in a military museum. Give me a hand with this mountain of knowledge. I want Gandhi, anywhere from three hundred to a thousand Earth-years ago.'

Hame came to life, started dragging out books. So did Colonel Shelton. Captain Grayder remained at his desk and continued to mourn the missing.

'Ah, here it is, four-seventy years back.' His Excellency ran a plump finger along the printed lines. 'Gandhi, sometimes called Bapu, or Father, Citizen of Hindi. Politico-philosopher.

Opposed authority by means of an ingenious system called civil disobedience. Last remnants disappeared with the Great Explosion, but may still persist on some planet out of contact.'

'Evidently it does,' commented Grayder, his voice dry. 'Civil disobedience,' repeated the ambassador, screwing up his eyes. He had the air of one trying to study something which was topsy-turvy. 'They can't make *that* a social basis. It just won't work.'

'It does work,' asserted Harrison, forgetting to put in the 'sir'.

'Are you contradicting me, mister?'

'I'm stating a fact.'

'Your Excellency,' Grayder began, 'I suggest – '

'Leave this to me.' His colour deepening, the ambassador waved him off. His gaze remained angrily on Harrison. 'You're very far from being an expert on socio-economic problems. Get that into your head, mister. Anyone of your calibre can be fooled by superficial appearances.'

'It works,' persisted Harrison, wondering where his own stubbornness was coming from.

'So does your tomfool bicycle. You've a bicycle mentality.'

Something snapped, and a voice remarkably like his own said, 'Nuts!' Astounded by this phenomenon, Harrison waggled his ears.

'What was that, mister?'

'Nuts!' he repeated, feeling that what has been done can't be undone.

Beating the purpling ambassador to the draw, Captain Grayder stood up and exercised his own authority.

'Regardless of further leave-quotas, if any, you are confined to the ship until further notice. Now get out!'

He went out, his mind in a whirl but his soul strangely satisfied. Outside, First Mate Morgan glowered at him.

'How long d'you think it's going to take me to work through this list of names when guys like you squat in there for a week?' He grunted with ire, cupped hands round his mouth and bellowed, 'Hope! Hope!'

No reply.

'Hope's been abandoned,' remarked a wit.

'That's funny,' sneered Morgan. 'Look at me shaking all

over.' He cupped again, tried the next name. 'Hyland! Hyland!'

No response.

Four more days, long, tedious, dragging ones. That made nine in all since the battleship formed the rut in which it was still sitting.

There was trouble on board. The third and fourth leave-quotas, put off repeatedly, were becoming impatient, irritable.

'Morgan showed him the third roster again this morning. Same result. Grayder admitted this world can't be defined as hostile and that we're entitled to run free.'

'Well, why the heck doesn't he keep to the book? The Space Commission could crucify him for disregarding it.'

'Same excuse. He says he's not denying leave, he's merely postponing it. That's a crafty evasion, isn't it? He says he'll grant it immediately the missing men come back.'

'That might be never. Darn him, he's using them as an excuse to gyp me out of my time.'

It was a strong and legitimate complaint. Weeks, months, years of close confinement in a constantly trembling bottle, no matter how large, demands ultimate release if only for a comparatively brief period. Men need fresh air, the good earth, the broad, clear-cut horizon, bulk-food, femininity, new faces.

'He *would* ram home the stopper just when we've learned the best way to get around. Civilian clothes and act like Gands, that's the secret. Even the first-quota boys are ready for another try.'

'Grayder daren't risk it. He's lost too many already. One more quota cut in half and he won't have enough crew to take off and get back. We'd be stuck here for keeps. How'd you like that?'

'I wouldn't grieve.'

'He could train the bureaucrats. Time those guys did some honest work.'

'It'd take three years. That's how long it took to train you, wasn't it?'

Harrison came along holding a small envelope. Three of them picked on him at sight.

'Look who sassed Hizonner and got confined to ship – same as us!'

'That's what I like about it,' Harrison observed. 'Better to get fastened down for something than for nothing.'

'It won't be long, you'll see! We're not going to hang around bellyaching for ever. Mighty soon we'll *do* something.'

'Such as what?'

'We're thinking it over,' evaded the other, not likely to be taken up so fast. He noticed the envelope. 'What have you got there? The day's mail?'

'Exactly that,' Harrison agreed.

'Have it your own way. I wasn't being nosey. I thought maybe you'd got some more snafu. You engineers usually pick up that paper-stuff first.'

'It *is* mail,' said Harrison.

'G'wan, nobody has letters in this neck of the cosmos.'

'I do.'

'How did you get it?'

'Worrall brought it from town an hour back. Friend of mine gave him dinner, let him bring the letter to kill the ob.' He pulled a large ear. 'Influence, that's what you boys need.'

Registering annoyance, one demanded, 'What's Worrall doing off the boat? Is he privileged?'

'Sort of. He's married, with three kids.'

'So what?'

'The ambassador figures that some people can be trusted more than others. They're not so likely to disappear, having too much to lose. So a few have been sorted out and sent into town to seek information about the missing men.'

'They found out anything?'

'Not much. Worrall says it's a waste of time. He found a few of our men here and there, tried to persuade them to return, but each said, "I won't." The Gands all said, "Myob". And that's that.'

'There must be something in it,' decided one of them, thoughtfully. 'I'd like to go see for myself.'

'That's what Grayder's afraid of.'

'We'll give him more than that to worry about if he doesn't become reasonable soon. Our patience is evaporating.'

'Mutinous talk,' Harrison reproved. He shook his head, looked sad. 'You shock me.'

He continued along the corridor, reached his own cabin, eyed the envelope. The writing inside might be feminine. He hoped so. He tore it open and had a look. It wasn't.

Signed by Gleed, the missive read, 'Never mind where I am or what I'm doing – this might get into the wrong hands. All I'll tell you is that I'll be fixed up topnotch providing I wait a decent interval to improve acquaintance. The rest of this concerns *you*.'

'Huh?' He leaned back on his bunk, held the letter nearer the light.

'I found a little fat guy running an empty shop. He just sits there, waiting. Next, I learn that he's established possession by occupation. He's doing it on behalf of a factory that makes two-ball rollers – those fan-driven cycles. They want someone to operate the place as a local roller sales and service depot. The little fat man has had four applications to date, but none with any engineering ability. The one who eventually gets this place will plant a functional-ob on the man, whatever that means. Anyway, this joint is yours for the taking. Don't be stupid. Jump in – the water's fine.'

'Zipping meteors!' said Harrison. His eyes travelled on to the bottom.

'P.S. Seth will give you the address. P.P.S. This burg is your brunette's home town and she's thinking of coming back. She wants to live near her sister – and so do I. Said sister is a honey!'

He stirred restlessly, read it through a second time, got up and paced around his tiny cabin. There were twelve hundred occupied worlds within the scope of the Empire. He'd seen about one-tenth of them. No spaceman could live long enough to get a look at the lot. The service was divided into cosmic groups, each dealing with its own sector.

Except by hearsay, of which there was plenty and most of it highly coloured, he would never know what heavens or pseudo-heavens existed in other sectors. In any case, it would be a blind gamble to pick an unfamiliar world for landbound life on someone else's recommendation. Not all think alike, or have the same tastes. One man's meat may be another man's poison.

The choice for retirement – which was the unlovely name for beginning another, different but vigorous life – was high-priced Terra or some more desirable planet in his own sector. There was the Epsilon group, fourteen of them, all attractive providing you could suffer the gravity and endure lumbering around like a tired elephant. There was Norton's Pink Heaven if, for the sake of getting by in peace, you could pander to Septimus Norton's rajah-complex and put up with his delusions of grandeur.

Up on the edge of the Milky Way was a matriarchy run by blonde Amazons, and a world of wizards, and a Pentecostal planet, and a globe where semisentient vegetables cultivated themselves under the direction of human masters; all scattered across forty light-years of space but readily accessible by Blieder-drive.

There were more than a hundred known to him by personal experience, though merely a tithe of the whole. All offered life and that company which is the essence of life. But this world, Gand, had something the others lacked. It had the quality of being present. It was part of the existing environment from which he drew data on which to build his decisions. The others were not. They lost virtue by being absent and faraway.

Unobtrusively, he made his way to the Blieder-room lockers, spent an hour cleaning and oiling his bicycle. Twilight was approaching when he returned. Taking a thin plaque from his pocket, he hung it on the wall, lay on his bunk and stared at it.

F – I. W.

The caller-system clicked, cleared its throat, announced, 'All personnel will stand by for general instructions at eight hours tomorrow.'

'I won't,' said Harrison. He closed his eyes.

Seven-twenty in the morning, but nobody thought it early. There is little sense of earliness or lateness among space-roamers – to regain it they have to be landbound a month, watching a sun rise and set.

The chartroom was empty but there was much activity in

the control cabin. Grayder was there with Shelton, Hame, Navigators Adamson, Werth and Yates and, of course, His Excellency.

'I never thought the day would come,' groused the latter, frowning at the star map over which the navigators pored. 'Less than a couple of weeks, and we get out, admitting defeat.'

'With all respect, your excellency, it doesn't look that way to me,' said Captain Grayder. 'One can be defeated only by enemies. These people are not enemies. That's precisely where they've got us by the short hairs. They're not definable as hostile.'

'That may be. I still say it's defeat. What else could you call it?'

'We've been outwitted by awkward relations. There's not much we can do about it. A man doesn't beat up his nieces and nephews merely because they won't speak to him.'

'That's your viewpoint as a ship's commander. You're confronted by a situation that requires you to go back to base and report. It's routine. The whole service is hidebound with routine.' The ambassador again eyed the star map as if he found it offensive. 'My own status is different. If I get out, it's a diplomatic defeat, an insult to the dignity and prestige of Terra. I'm far from sure that I ought to go. It might be better if I stayed put – though that would give them the chance to offer further insults.'

'I would not presume to advise you what to do for the best,' Grayder said. 'All I know is this: we carry troops and armaments for any policing or protective purposes that might be found necessary here. But I can't use them offensively against these Gands because they've provided no pretext and because, in any case, our full strength isn't enough to crush twelve million of them. We need an armada for that. We'd be fighting at the extreme of our reach – and the reward of victory would be a useless world.'

'Don't remind me. I've stewed it until I'm sick of it.'

Grayder shrugged. He was a man of action so long as it was action in space. Planetary shenanigans were not properly his pigeon. Now that the decisive moment was drawing near, when he would be back in his own attenuated element, he was becoming phlegmatic. To him, Gand was a visit among a hundred such, with plenty more to come.

'Your excellency, if you're in serious doubt whether to remain or come with us, I'd be favoured if you'd reach a decision fairly soon. Morgan has given me the tip that if I haven't approved the third leave-quota by ten o'clock the men are going to take matters into their own hands and walk off.'

'That would get them into trouble of a really hot kind, wouldn't it?'

'Some,' agreed Captain Grayder, 'but not so hot. They intend to turn my own quibbling against me. Since I have not officially forbidden leave, a walk-out won't be mutiny. I've merely been postponing leave. They could plead before the Space Commission that I've deliberately ignored regulations. They might get away with it if the members were in the mood to assert their authority.'

'The Commission ought to be taken on a few long flights,' opined His Excellency. 'They'd discover some things they'll never learn behind a desk.' He eyed the other in mock hopefulness. 'Any chance of accidentally dropping our cargo of bureaucrats overboard on the way back? A misfortune like that might benefit the spaceways, if not humanity.'

'That idea strikes me as Gandish,' observed Grayder.

'They wouldn't think of it. Their technique is to say no, no, a thousand times no. That's all – but judging by what has happened here, it is enough.' The ambassador pondered his predicament, reached a decision. 'I'm coming with you. It goes against the grain because it smacks of surrender. To stay would be a defiant gesture, but I've got to face the fact that it won't serve any useful purpose at the present stage.'

'Very well, your excellency.' Grayder went to a port, looked through it towards the town. 'I'm down about four hundred men. Some of them have deserted, for keeps. The rest will come back if I wait long enough. They've struck it lucky, got their legs under somebody's table and gone AWOL and they're likely to extend their time for as long as the fun lasts on the principle that they may as well be hung for sheep as lambs. I get that sort of trouble on every long trip. It's not so bad on short ones.' A pause while moodily he surveyed a terrain bare of returning prodigals. 'But we can't wait for them. Not here.'

'No, I reckon not.'

'If we hang around any longer, we're going to lose another hundred or two. There won't be enough skilled men to take the boat up. Only way I can beat them to the draw is to give the order to prepare for take-off. They all come under flight-regulations from that moment.' He registered a lopsided smile. 'That will give the space lawyers something to think about!'

'As soon as you like,' approved the ambassador. He joined the other at the port, studied the distant road, watched three Gand coaches whirl along it without stopping. He frowned, still upset by the type of mind which insists on pretending that a mountain isn't there. His attention shifted sidewise, towards the tail-end. He stiffened and said, 'What are those men doing outside?'

Shooting a swift glance in the same direction, Grayder grabbed the caller-mike and rapped, 'All personnel will prepare for take-off at once!' Juggling a couple of switches, he changed lines, said, 'Who is that? Sergeant-Major Bidworthy? Look, sergeant-major, there are half a dozen men beyond the midship lock. Get them in immediately – we're lifting as soon as everything's ready.'

The fore and aft gangways had been rolled into their stowage spaces long before. Some fast-thinking quartermaster prevented further escapes by operating the midship ladder-wind, thus trapping Bidworthy along with more would-be deserters.

Finding himself stalled, Bidworthy stood in the rim of the lock and glared at those outside. His moustache not only bridled, but quivered. Five of the offenders had been members of the first leave-quota. One of them was a trooper. That got his rag out, a trooper. The sixth was Harrison, complete with bicycle polished and shining.

Searing the lot of them, the trooper in particular, Bidworthy rasped, 'Get back on board. No arguments. No funny business. We're taking off.'

'Hear that?' asked one, nudging the nearest. 'Get back on board. If you can't jump thirty feet, you'd better flap your arms and fly.'

'No sauce from you,' roared Bidworthy. 'I've got my orders.'

'He takes orders,' remarked the trooper. 'At his age.'

'Can't understand it,' commented another, shaking a sorrowful head.

Bidworthy scrabbled the lock's smooth rim in vain search of something to grasp. A ridge, a knob, a projection of some sort was needed to take the strain.

'I warn you men that if you try me too – '

'Save your breath, Biddy,' interjected the trooper. 'From now on, I'm a Gand.' With that, he turned and walked rapidly towards the road, four following.

Getting astride his bike, Harrison put a foot on a pedal. His back tyre promptly sank with a loud *whee-e-e*.

'Come back!' howled Bidworthy at the retreating five. He made extravagant motions, tried to tear the ladder from its automatic grips. A siren keened thinly inside the vessel. That upped his agitation by several ergs.

'Hear that?' With vein-pulsing ire, he watched Harrison tighten the rear valve and apply his hand pump. 'We're about to lift. For the last time – '

Again the siren, this time in a quick series of shrill toots. Bidworthy jumped backward as the seal came down. The lock closed. Harrison again mounted his machine, settled a foot on a pedal but remained watching.

The metal monster shivered from nose to tail then rose slowly and in utter silence. There was stately magnificence in the ascent of such enormous bulk. It increased its rate of climb gradually, went faster, faster, became a toy, a dot and finally disappeared.

For just a moment, Harrison felt a touch of doubt, a hint of regret. It soon passed away. He glanced towards the road.

The five self-elected Gands had thumbed a coach which was picking them up. That was co-operation apparently precipitated by the ship's disappearance. Quick on the uptake these people. He saw it move off on huge rubber balls bearing the five with it. A fan-cycle raced in the opposite direction, hummed into the distance.

'Your brunette,' Gleed had described her. What gave him that idea? Had she made some remark which he'd construed as complimentary because it made no reference to outsize ears?

He had a last look around. The earth to his left bore a great curved rut one mile long by twelve feet deep. Two thousand Terrans had been there.

Then about eighteen hundred.

Then sixteen hundred.

Less five.

'One left – me!' he said to himself.

Giving a fatalistic shrug, he put the pressure on and rode to town.

And then there were none.

PROFESSION

by Isaac Asimov

George Platen could not conceal the longing in his voice. It was too much to suppress. He said, 'Tomorrow's the first of May. Olympics!'

He rolled over on his stomach and peered over the foot of his bed at his room-mate. Didn't *he* feel it, too? Didn't *this* make some impression on him?

George's face was thin and had grown a trifle thinner in the nearly year and a half that he had been at the House. His figure was slight but the look in his blue eyes was as intense as it had ever been, and right now there was a trapped look in the way his fingers curled against the bedspread.

George's room-mate looked up briefly from his book and took the opportunity to adjust the light-level of the stretch of wall near his chair. His name was Hali Omani and he was a Nigerian by birth. His dark brown skin and massive features seemed made for calmness, and mention of the Olympics did not move him.

He said, 'I know, George.'

George owed much to Hali's patience and kindness when it was needed, but even patience and kindness could be over-done. Was this a time to sit there like a statue built of some dark, warm wood?

George wondered if he himself would grow like that after ten years here and rejected the thought violently. No!

He said defiantly, 'I think you've forgotten what May means.'

The other said, 'I remember very well what it means. It means nothing! You're the one who's forgotten that. May means nothing to you, George Platen, and,' he added softly, 'it means nothing to me, Hali Omani.'

George said, 'The ships are coming in for recruits. By June, thousands and thousands will leave with millions of men and women heading for any world you can name, and all that means nothing?'

'Less than nothing. What do you want me to do about it, anyway?' Omani ran his finger along a difficult passage in the book he was reading and his lips moved soundlessly.

George watched him. Damn it, he thought, yell, scream; you can do that much. Kick at me, do anything.

It was only that he wanted not to be so alone in his anger. He wanted not to be the only one so filled with resentment, not to be the only one dying a slow death.

It was better those first weeks when the Universe was a small shell of vague light and sound pressing down upon him. It was better before Omani had wavered into view and dragged him back to a life that wasn't worth living.

Omani! He was old! He was at least thirty. George thought: Will I be like that at thirty? Will I be like that in twelve years?

And because he was afraid he might be, he yelled at Omani, 'Will you stop reading that fool book?'

Omani turned a page and read on a few words, then lifted his head with its skull-cap of crisply curled hair and said, 'What?'

'What good does it do you to read the book?' He stepped forward, snorted 'More electronics', and slapped it out of Omani's hands.

Omani got up slowly and picked up the book. He smoothed a crumpled page without visible rancour. 'Call it the satisfaction of curiosity,' he said. 'I understand a little of it today, perhaps a little more tomorrow. That's a victory in a way.'

'A victory. What kind of a victory? Is that what satisfies you in life? To get to know enough to be a quarter of a Registered Electronician by the time you're sixty-five?'

'Perhaps by the time I'm thirty-five.'

'And then who'll want you? Who'll use you? Where will you go?'

'No one. No one. Nowhere. I'll stay here and read other books.'

'And that satisfies you? Tell me! You've dragged me to class. You've got me to reading and memorizing too. For what? There's nothing in it that satisfies me.'

'What good will it do you to deny yourself satisfaction?'

'It means I'll quit the whole farce. I'll do as I planned to do in the beginning before you dovey-lovied me out of it. I'm going to force them to – to – '

Omani put down his book. He let the other run down and then said, 'To what, George?'

'To correct a miscarriage of justice. A frame-up. I'll get that Antonelli and force him to admit he – he – '

Omani shook his head. 'Everyone who comes here insists it's a mistake. I thought you'd passed that stage.'

'Don't call it a stage,' said George violently. 'In my case, it's a fact. I've told you – '

'You've told me, but in your heart you know no one made any mistake as far as you were concerned.'

'Because no one will admit it? You think any of them would admit a mistake unless they were forced to? – Well, I'll force them.'

It was May that was doing this to George; it was Olympics month. He felt it bring the old wildness back and he couldn't stop it. He didn't want to stop it. He had been in danger of forgetting.

He said, 'I was going to be a Computer Programmer and I *can* be one. I could be one today, regardless of what they say analysis shows.' He pounded his mattress. 'They're wrong. They *must* be.'

'The analysts are never wrong.'

'They *must* be. Do you doubt my intelligence?'

'Intelligence hasn't one thing to do with it. Haven't you been told that often enough? Can't you understand that?'

George rolled away, lay on his back, and stared sombrely at the ceiling.

'What did you want to be, Hali?'

'I had no fixed plans. Hydroponicist would have suited me, I suppose.'

'Did you think you could make it?'

'I wasn't sure.'

George had never asked personal questions of Omani before. It struck him as queer, almost unnatural, that other people had had ambitions and ended here. Hydroponicist!

He said, 'Did you think you'd make *this*?'

'No, but here I am just the same.'

'And you're satisfied. Really, really satisfied. You're happy. You love it. You wouldn't be anywhere else.'

Slowly, Omani got to his feet. Carefully, he began to unmake his bed. He said, 'George, you're a hard case. You're knocking yourself out because you won't accept the facts about yourself. George, you're here in what you call the House, but I've never heard you give it its full title. Say it, George, say it. Then go to bed and sleep this off.'

George gritted his teeth and showed them. He choked out, 'No!'

'Then I will,' said Omani, and he did. He shaped each syllable carefully.

George was bitterly ashamed at the sound of it. He turned his head away.

For most of the first eighteen years of his life, George Platen had headed firmly in one direction, that of Registered Computer Programmer. There were those in his crowd who spoke wisely of Spationautics, Refrigeration Technology, Transportation Control, and even Administration. But George held firm.

He argued relative merits as vigorously as any of them, and why not? Education Day loomed ahead of them and was the great fact of their existence. It approached steadily, as fixed and certain as the calendar – the first day of November of the year following one's eighteenth birthday.

After that day, there were other topics of conversation. One could discuss with others some detail of the profession, or the virtues of one's wife and children, or the fate of one's space-polo team, or one's experiences in the Olympics. Before Education Day, however, there was only one topic that unfailingly and unwearyingly held everyone's interest, and that was Education Day.

'What are you going for? Think you'll make it? Heck, that's no good. Look at the records; quota's been cut. Logistics now –'

Or Hypermechanics now – Or Communications now – Or Gravitics now –

Especially Gravitics at the moment. Everyone had been talking about Gravitics in the few years just before George's

Education Day because of the development of the Gravitic power engine.

Any world within ten light-years of a dwarf star, everyone said, would give its eyeteeth for any kind of Registered Gravitics Engineer.

The thought of that never bothered George. Sure it would; all the eyeteeth it could scare up. But George had also heard what had happened before in a newly developed technique. Rationalization and simplification followed in a flood. New models each year; new types of gravitic engines; new principles. Then all those eyeteeth gentlemen would find themselves out of date and superseded by later models with later educations. The first group would then have to settle down to unskilled labour or ship out to some backwoods world that wasn't quite caught up yet.

Now Computer Programmers were in steady demand year after year, century after century. The demand never reached wild peaks; there was never a howling bull market for Programmers; but the demand climbed steadily as new worlds opened up and as older worlds grew more complex.

He had argued with Stubby Trevelyan about that constantly. As best friends, their arguments had to be constant and vitriolic and, of course, neither ever persuaded or was persuaded.

But then Trevelyan had had a father who was a Registered Metallurgist and had actually served on one of the Outworlds, and a grandfather who had also been a Registered Metallurgist. He himself was intent on becoming a Registered Metallurgist almost as a matter of family right and was firmly convinced that any other profession was a shade less than respectable.

'There'll always be metal,' he said, 'and there's an accomplishment in moulding alloys to specification and watching structures grow. Now what's a Programmer going to be doing? Sitting at a coder all day long, feeding some fool mile-long machine.'

Even at sixteen, George had learned to be practical. He said simply, 'There'll be a million Metallurgists put out along with you.'

'Because it's good. A good profession. The best.'

'But you get crowded out, Stubby. You can be way back in line. Any world can tape out its own Metallurgists, and the market for advanced Earth models isn't so big. And it's mostly the small worlds that want them. You know what per cent of the turnout of Registered Metallurgists get tabbed for worlds with a Grade A rating. I looked it up. It's just 13.3 per cent. That means you'll have seven chances in eight of being stuck in some world that just about has running water. You may even be stuck on Earth; 2.3 per cent are.'

Trevelyan said belligerently, 'There's no disgrace in staying on Earth. Earth needs technicians, too. Good ones.' His grandfather had been an Earth-bound Metallurgist, and Trevelyan lifted his finger to his upper lip and dabbed at an as yet non-existent moustache.

George knew about Trevelyan's grandfather and, considering the Earth-bound position of his own ancestry, was in no mood to sneer. He said diplomatically, 'Not intellectual disgrace. Of course not. But it's nice to get into a Grade A world, isn't it?

'Now you take Programmers. Only the Grade A worlds have the kind of computers that really need first-class Programmers so they're the only ones in the market. And Programmer tapes are complicated and hardly any one fits. They need more Programmers than their own population can supply. It's just a matter of statistics. There's one first-class Programmer per million, say. A world needs twenty and has a population of ten million, they have to come to Earth for five to fifteen Programmers. Right?

'And you know how many Registered Computer Programmers went to Grade A planets last year? I'll tell you. Every last one. If you're a Programmer, you're a picked man. Yes, sir.'

Trevelyan frowned. 'If only one in a million makes it, what makes you think *you*'ll make it?'

George said guardedly, 'I'll make it.'

He never dared tell anyone; not Trevelyan; not his parents; of exactly what he was doing that made him so confident. But he wasn't worried. He was simply confident (that was the worst of the memories he had in the hopeless days afterwards). He was as blandly confident as the average eight-year-old kid

107

approaching Reading Day – that childhood preview of Education Day.

Of course, Reading Day had been different. Partly, there was the simple fact of childhood. A boy of eight takes many extraordinary things in his stride. One day you can't read and the next day you can. That's just the way things are. Like the sun shining.

And then not so much depended upon it. There were no recruiters just ahead, waiting and jostling for the lists and scores on the coming Olympics. A boy or girl who goes through the Reading Day is just someone who has ten more years of undifferentiated living upon Earth's crawling surface; just someone who returns to his family with one new ability.

By the time Education Day came, ten years later, George wasn't even sure of most of the details of his own Reading Day.

Most clearly of all, he remembered it to be a dismal September day with a mild rain falling. (September for Reading Day; November for Education Day; May for Olympics. They made nursery rhymes out of it.) George had dressed by the wall lights, with his parents far more excited than he himself was. His father was a Registered Pipe Fitter and had found his occupation on Earth. This fact had always been a humiliation to him, although, of course, as anyone could see plainly, most of each generation must stay on Earth in the nature of things.

There had to be farmers and miners and even technicians on Earth. It was only the late-model, high-specialty professions that were in demand on the Outworlds, and only a few millions a year out of Earth's eight billion population could be exported. Every man and woman on Earth couldn't be among that group.

But every man and woman could hope that at least one of his children could be one, and Platen, Senior, was certainly no exception. It was obvious to him (and, to be sure, to others as well) that George was notably intelligent and quick-minded. He would be bound to do well and he would have to, as he was an only child. If George didn't end on an Outworld, they would have to wait for grandchildren before a next chance would come along, and that was too far in the future to be much consolation.

Reading Day would not prove much, of course, but it would be the only indication they would have before the big day itself. Every parent on Earth would be listening to the quality of reading when his child came home with it; listening for any particularly easy flow of words and building that into certain omens of the future. There were few families that didn't have at least one hopeful who, from Reading Day on, was the great hope because of the way he handled his trisyllabics.

Dimly, George was aware of the cause of his parents' tension, and if there was any anxiety in his young heart that drizzly morning, it was only the fear that his father's hopeful expression might fade out when he returned home with his reading.

The children met in the large assembly room of the town's Education hall. All over Earth, in millions of local halls, throughout that month, similar groups of children would be meeting. George felt depressed by the greyness of the room and by the other children, strained and stiff in unaccustomed finery.

Automatically, George did as all the rest of the children did. He found the small clique that represented the children of his floor of the apartment house and joined them.

Trevelyan, who lived immediately next door, still wore his hair childishly long and was years removed from the sideburns and thin, reddish moustache that he was to grow as soon as he was physiologically capable of it.

Trevelyan (to whom George was then known as Jaw-jee) said, 'Bet you're scared.'

'I am not,' said George. Then, confidentially, 'My folks got a hunk of printing up on the dresser in my room, and when I come home, I'm going to read it for them.' (George's main suffering at the moment lay in the fact that he didn't quite know where to put his hands. He had been warned not to scratch his head or rub his ears or pick his nose or put his hands into his pockets. This eliminated almost every possibility.)

Trevelyan put *his* hands in his pockets and said, 'My father isn't worried.'

Trevelyan, Senior, had been a Metallurgist on Diporia for nearly seven years, which gave him a superior social status in his neighbourhood even though he had retired and returned to Earth.

Earth discouraged these re-immigrants because of population problems, but a small trickle did return. For one thing the cost of living was lower on Earth, and what was a trifling annuity on Diporia, say, was a comfortable income on Earth. Besides, there were always men who found more satisfaction in displaying their success before the friends and scenes of their childhood than before all the rest of the Universe besides.

Trevelyan, Senior, further explained that if he stayed on Diporia, so would his children, and Diporia was a one-spaceship world. Back on Earth, his kids could end anywhere, even Novia.

Stubby Trevelyan had picked up that item early. Even before Reading Day, his conversation was based on the carelessly assumed fact that his ultimate home would be in Novia.

George, oppressed by thoughts of the other's future greatness and his own small-time contrast, was driven to belligerent defence at once.

'My father isn't worried either. He just wants to hear me read because he knows I'll be good. I suppose your father would just as soon not hear you because he knows you'll be all wrong.'

'I will not be all wrong. Reading is *nothing*. On Novia, I'll *hire* people to read to me.'

'Because *you* won't be able to read yourself, on account of you're *dumb*!'

'Then how come I'll be on Novia?'

And George, driven, made the great denial, 'Who says you'll be on Novia? Bet you don't go anywhere.'

Stubby Trevelyan reddened. 'I won't be a Pipe Fitter like your old man.'

'Take that back, you dumbhead.'

'You take *that* back.'

They stood nose to nose, not wanting to fight but relieved at having something familiar to do in this strange place. Furthermore, now that George had curled his hands into fists and lifted them before his face, the problem of what to do with his hands was, at least temporarily, solved. Other children gathered round excitedly.

But then it all ended when a woman's voice sounded loudly over the public address system. There was instant silence everywhere. George dropped his fists and forgot Trevelyan.

'Children,' said the voice, 'we are going to call out your names. As each child is called, he or she is to go to one of the men waiting along the side walls. Do you see them? They are wearing red uniforms so they will be easy to find. The girls will go to the right. The boys will go to the left. Now look about and see which man in red is nearest to you – '

George found his man at a glance and waited for his name to be called off. He had not been introduced before this to the sophistications of the alphabet, and the length of time it took to reach his own name grew disturbing.

The crowd of children thinned; little rivulets made their way to each of the red-clad guides.

When the name 'George Platen' was finally called, his sense of relief was exceeded only by the feeling of pure gladness at the fact that Stubby Trevelyan still stood in his place, un-called.

George shouted back over his shoulder as he left, 'Yay, Stubby, maybe they don't want you.'

That moment of gaiety quickly left. He was herded into a line and directed down corridors in the company of strange children. They all looked at one another, large-eyed and concerned, but beyond a snuffling, 'Quitcher pushing' and 'Hey, watch out' there was no conversation.

They were handed little slips of paper which they were told must remain with them. George stared at his curiously. Little black marks of different shapes. He knew it to be printing but how could anyone make words out of it? He couldn't imagine.

He was told to strip; he and four other boys who were all that now remained together. All the new clothes came shucking off and four eight-year-olds stood naked and small, shivering more out of embarrassment than cold. Medical technicians came past, probing them, testing them with odd instruments, pricking them for blood. Each took the little cards and made additional marks on them with little black rods that produced the marks, all neatly lined up, with great speed. George stared at the new marks, but they were no more comprehensible than the old. The children were ordered back into their clothes.

They sat on separate little chairs then and waited again. Names were called again and 'George Platen' came third.

He moved into a large room, filled with frightening instruments with knobs and glassy panels in front. There was a desk in the very centre, and behind it a man sat, his eyes on the papers piled before him.

He said, 'George Platen?'

'Yes, sir,' said George, in a shaky whisper. All this waiting and all this going here and there was making him nervous. He wished it were over.

The man behind the desk said, 'I am Dr Lloyd, George. How are you?'

The doctor didn't look up as he spoke. It was as though he had said those words over and over again and didn't have to look up any more.

'I'm all right.'

'Are you afraid, George?'

'N – no, sir,' said George, sounding afraid even in his own ears.

'That's good,' said the doctor, 'because there's nothing to be afraid of, you know. Let's see, George. It says here on your card that your father is named Peter and that he's a Registered Pipe Fitter and your mother is named Amy and is a Registered Home Technician. Is that right?'

'Y – yes, sir.'

'And your birthday is February 13, and you had an ear infection about a year ago. Right?'

'Yes, sir.'

'Do you know how I know all these things?'

'It's on the card, I think, sir.'

'That's right.' The doctor looked up at George for the first time and smiled. He showed even teeth and looked much younger than George's father. Some of George's nervousness vanished.

The doctor passed the card to George. 'Do you know what all those things there mean, George?'

Although George knew he did not he was startled by the sudden request into looking at the card as though he might understand now through some sudden stroke of fate. But they were just marks as before and he passed the card back. 'No, sir.'

'Why not?'

George felt a sudden pang of suspicion concerning the sanity of his doctor. Didn't he know why not?

George said, 'I can't read, sir.'

'Would you like to read?'

'Yes, sir.'

'Why, George?'

George stared, appalled. No one had ever asked him that. He had no answer. He said falteringly, 'I don't know, sir.'

'Printed information will direct you all through your life. There is so much you'll have to know even after Education Day. Cards like this one will tell you. Books will tell you. Television screens will tell you. Printing will tell you such useful things and such interesting things that not being able to read would be as bad as not being able to see. Do you understand?'

'Yes, sir.'

'Are you afraid, George?'

'No, sir.'

'Good. Now I'll tell you exactly what we'll do first. I'm going to put these wires on your forehead just over the corners of your eyes. They'll stick there but they won't hurt at all. Then, I'll turn on something that will make a buzz. It will sound funny and it may tickle you, but it won't hurt. Now if it does hurt, you tell me, and I'll turn it off right away, but it won't hurt. All right?'

George nodded and swallowed.

'Are you ready?'

George nodded. He closed his eyes while the doctor busied himself. His parents had explained this to him. They, too, had said it wouldn't hurt, but then there were always the older children. There were the ten- and twelve-year-olds who howled after the eight-year-olds waiting for Reading Day, 'Watch out for the needle.' There were the others who took you off in confidence and said, 'They got to cut your head open. They use a sharp knife that big with a hook on it', and so on into horrifying details.

113

George had never believed them but he had had nightmares, and now he closed his eyes and felt pure terror.

He didn't feel the wires at his temple. The buzz was a distant thing, and there was the sound of his own blood in his ears, ringing hollowly as though it and he were in a large cave. Slowly he chanced opening his eyes.

The doctor had his back to him. From one of the instruments a strip of paper unwound and was covered with a thin, wavy purple line. The doctor tore off pieces and put them into a slot in another machine. He did it over and over again. Each time a little piece of film came out, which the doctor looked at. Finally, he turned towards George with a queer frown between his eyes.

The buzzing stopped.

George said breathlessly, 'Is it over?'

The doctor said, 'Yes,' but he was still frowning.

'Can I read now?' asked George. He felt no different.

The doctor said, 'What?' then smiled very suddenly and briefly. He said, 'It works fine, George. You'll be reading in fifteen minutes. Now we're going to use another machine this time and it will take longer. I'm going to cover your whole head, and when I turn it on you won't be able to see or hear anything for a while, but it won't hurt. Just to make sure I'm going to give you a little switch to hold in your hand. If anything hurts, you press the little button and everything shuts off. All right?'

In later years, George was told that the little switch was strictly a dummy; that it was introduced solely for confidence. He never did know for sure, however, since he never pushed the button.

A large smoothly curved helmet with a rubbery inner lining was placed over his head and left there. Three or four little knobs seemed to grab at him and bite into his skull, but there was only a little pressure that faded. No pain.

The doctor's voice sounded dimly. 'Everything all right, George?'

And then, with no real warning, a layer of thick felt closed down all about him. He was disembodied, there was no sensation, no universe, only himself and a distant murmur at the very ends of nothingness telling him something – telling him – telling him –

He strained to hear and understand but there was all that thick felt between.

Then the helmet was taken off his head, and the light was so bright that it hurt his eyes while the doctor's voice drummed at his ears.

The doctor said, 'Here's your card, George. What does it say?'

George looked at his card again and gave out a strangled shout. The marks weren't just marks at all. They made up words. They were words just as clearly as though something were whispering them in his ears. He could *hear* them being whispered as he looked at them.

'What does it say, George?'

'It says – it says – "Platen, George. Born 13 February 6492 of Peter and Amy Platen in . . ." ' He broke off.

'You can read, George,' said the doctor. 'It's all over.'

'For good? I won't forget how?'

'Of course not.' The doctor leaned over to shake hands gravely. 'You will be taken home now.'

It was days before George got over this new and great talent of his. He read for his father with such facility that Platen, Senior, wept and called relatives to tell the good news.

George walked about town, reading every scrap of printing he could find and wondering how it was that none of it had ever made sense to him before.

He tried to remember how it was not to be able to read and he couldn't. As far as his feeling about it was concerned, he had always been able to read. Always.

At eighteen, George was rather dark, of medium height, but thin enough to look taller. Trevelyan, who was scarcely an inch shorter, had a stockiness of build that made 'Stubby' more than ever appropriate, but in his last year he had grown self-conscious. The nickname could no longer be used without reprisal. And since Trevelyan disapproved of his proper first name even more strongly, he was called Trevelyan or any decent variant of that. As though to prove his manhood further, he had most persistently grown a pair of sideburns and a bristly moustache.

He was sweating and nervous now, and George, who had himself grown out of 'Jaw-jee' and into the curt monosyllabic gutturality of 'George', was rather amused by that.

They were in the same large hall they had been in ten years before (and not since). It was as if a vague dream of the past had come to sudden reality. In the first few minutes George had been distinctly surprised at finding everything seem smaller and more cramped than his memory told him; then he made allowance for his own growth.

The crowd was smaller than it had been in childhood. It was exclusively male this time. The girls had another day assigned them.

Trevelyan leaned over to say, 'Beats me the way they make you wait.'

'Red tape,' said George. 'You can't avoid it.'

Trevelyan said, 'What makes *you* so damned tolerant about it?'

'I've got nothing to worry about.'

'Oh, brother, you make me sick. I hope you end up Registered Manure Spreader just so I can see your face when you do.' His sombre eyes swept the crowd anxiously.

George looked about, too. It wasn't quite the system they used on the children. Matters went slower, and instructions had been given out at the start in print (an advantage over the pre-Readers). The names Platen and Trevelyan were well down the alphabet still, but this time the two knew it.

Young men came out of the education rooms, frowning and uncomfortable, picked up their clothes and belongings, then went off to analysis to learn the results.

Each, as he came out, would be surrounded by a clot of the thinning crowd. 'How was it?' 'How'd it feel?' 'Whacha think ya made?' 'Ya feel any different?'

Answers were vague and noncommittal.

George forced himself to remain out of those clots. You only raised your own blood pressure. Everyone said you stood the best chance if you remained calm. Even so, you could feel the palms of your hands grow cold. Funny that new tensions came with the years.

For instance, high-specialty professionals heading out for an Outworld were accompanied by a wife (or husband). It was important to keep the sex ratio in good balance on all worlds. And if you were going out to a Grade A world, what girl would refuse you? George had no specific girl in mind yet; he wanted none. Not now! Once he made Programmer; once he could add to his name, Registered Computer Programmer, he could take his pick, like a sultan in a harem. The thought excited him and he tried to put it away. Must stay calm.

Trevelyan muttered, 'What's it all about anyway? First they say it works best if you're relaxed and at ease. Then they put you through this and make it impossible for you to be relaxed and at ease.'

'Maybe that's the idea. They're separating the boys from the men to begin with. Take it easy, Trev.'

'Shut up.'

George's turn came. His name was not called. It appeared in glowing letters on the notice-board.

He waved at Trevelyan. 'Take it easy. Don't let it get you.'

He was happy as he entered the testing chamber. Actually happy.

The man behind the desk said, 'George Platen?'

For a fleeting instant there was a razor-sharp picture in George's mind of another man, ten years earlier, who had asked the same question, and it was almost as though this were the same man and he, George, had turned eight again as he had stepped across the threshold.

But the man looked up and, of course, the face matched that of the sudden memory not at all. The nose was bulbous, the hair thin and stringy, and the chin wattled as though its owner had once been grossly overweight and had reduced.

The man behind the desk looked annoyed. 'Well?'

George came to Earth. 'I'm George Platen, sir.'

'Say so, then. I'm Dr Zachary Antonelli, and we're going to be intimately acquainted in a moment.'

He stared at small strips of film, holding them up to the light owlishly.

George winced inwardly. Very hazily, he remembered that other doctor (he had forgotten the name) staring at such film. Could these be the same? The other doctor had frowned and

117

this one was looking at him now as though he were angry.

His happiness was already just about gone.

Dr Antonelli spread the pages of a thickish file out before him now and put the films carefully to one side. 'It says here you want to be a Computer Programmer.'

'Yes, doctor.'

'Still do?'

'Yes, sir.'

'It's a responsible and exacting position. Do you feel up to it?'

'Yes, sir.'

'Most pre-Educates don't put down any specific profession. I believe they are afraid of queering it.'

'I think that's right, sir.'

'Aren't you afraid of that?'

'I might as well be honest, sir.'

Dr Antonelli nodded but without any noticeable lightening of his expression. 'Why do you want to be a Programmer?'

'It's a responsible and exacting position as you said, sir. It's an important job and an exciting one. I like it and I think I can do it.'

Dr Antonelli put the papers away, and looked at George sourly. He said, 'How do you know you like it? Because you think you'll be snapped up by some Grade A planet?'

George thought uneasily: He's trying to rattle you. Stay calm and stay frank.

He said, 'I think a Programmer has a good chance, sir, but even if I were left on Earth, I know I'd like it.' (That was true enough. I'm not lying, thought George.)

'All right, how do you know?'

He asked it as though he knew there was no decent answer and George almost smiled. He had one.

He said, 'I've been reading about Programming, sir.'

'You've been *what*?' Now the doctor looked genuinely astonished and George took pleasure in that.

'Reading about it, sir. I bought a book on the subject and I've been studying it.'

'A book for Registered Programmers?'

'Yes, sir.'

'But you couldn't understand it.'

'Not at first. I got other books on mathematics and electronics. I made out all I could. I still don't know much, but I know enough to know I like it and to know I can make it.' (Even his parents never found that secret cache of books or knew why he spent so much time in his own room or exactly what happened to the sleep he missed.)

The doctor pulled at the loose skin under his chin. 'What was your idea in doing that, son?'

'I wanted to make sure I would be interested, sir.'

'Surely you know that being interested means nothing. You could be devoured by a subject and if the physical make-up of your brain makes it more efficient for you to be something else, something else you will be. You know that, don't you?'

'I've been told that,' said George cautiously.

'Well, believe it. It's true.'

George said nothing.

Dr Antonelli said, 'Or do you believe that studying some subject will bend the brain cells in that direction, like that other theory that a pregnant woman need only listen to great music persistently to make a composer of her child? Do you believe that?'

George flushed. That had certainly been in his mind. By forcing his intellect constantly in the desired direction, he had felt sure that he would be getting a head start. Most of his confidence had rested on exactly that point.

'I never – ' he began, and found no way of finishing.

'Well, it isn't true. Good Lord, youngster, your brain pattern is fixed at birth. It can be altered by a blow hard enough to damage the cells or by a burst blood vessel or by a tumour or by a major infection – each time, of course, for the worse. But it certainly can't be affected by your thinking special thoughts.' He stared at George thoughtfully, then said, 'Who told you to do this?'

George, now thoroughly disturbed, swallowed and said, 'No one, doctor. My own idea.'

'Who knew you were doing it after you started?'

'No one. Doctor, I meant to do no wrong.'

'Who said anything about wrong? Useless is what I would say. Why did you keep it to yourself?'

'I – I thought they'd laugh at me.' (He thought abruptly of

a recent exchange with Trevelyan. George had very cautiously broached the thought, as of something merely circulating distantly in the very outermost reaches of his mind, concerning the possibility of learning something by ladling it into the mind by hand, so to speak, in bits and pieces. Trevelyan had hooted, 'George, you'll be tanning your own shoes next and weaving your own shirts.' He had been thankful then for his policy of secrecy.)

Dr Antonelli shoved the bits of film he had first looked at from position to position in morose thought. Then he said, 'Let's get you analysed. This is getting me nowhere.'

The wires went to George's temples. There was the buzzing. Again there came a sharp memory of ten years ago.

George's hands were clammy; his heart pounded. He should never have told the doctor about his secret reading.

It was his damned vanity, he told himself. He had wanted to show how enterprising he was, how full of initiative. Instead, he had showed himself superstitious and ignorant and aroused the hostility of the doctor. (He could tell the doctor hated him for a wise guy on the make.)

And now he had brought himself to such a state of nervousness, he was sure the analyser would show nothing that made sense.

He wasn't aware of the moment when the wires were removed from his temples. The sight of the doctor, staring at him thoughtfully, blinked into his consciousness and that was that; the wires were gone. George dragged himself together with a tearing effort. He had quite given up his ambition to be a Programmer. In the space of ten minutes, it had all gone.

He said dismally, 'I suppose no?'

'No what?'

'No Programmer?'

The doctor rubbed his nose and said, 'You get your clothes and whatever belongs to you and go to room 15-C. Your files will be waiting for you there. So will my report.'

George said in complete surprise 'Have I been Educated already? I thought this was just to – '

Dr Antonelli stared down at his desk. 'It will all be explained to you. You do as I say.'

George felt something like panic. What was it they couldn't tell him? He wasn't fit for anything but Registered Labourer. They were going to prepare him for that; adjust him to it.

He was suddenly certain of it and he had to keep from screaming by main force.

He stumbled back to his place of waiting. Trevelyan was not there, a fact for which he would have been thankful if he had had enough self-possession to be meaningfully aware of his surroundings. Hardly anyone was left, in fact, and the few who were looked as though they might ask him questions were it not that they were too worn out by their tail-of-the-alphabet waiting to buck the fierce, hot look of anger and hate he cast at them.

What right had *they* to be technicians and he, himself, a Labourer? Labourer! He was *certain*!

He was led by a red-uniformed guide along the busy corridors lined with separate rooms each containing its groups, here two, there five: the Motor Mechanics, the Construction Engineers, the Agronomists – There were hundreds of specialized Professions and most of them would be represented in this small town by one or two anyway.

He hated them all just then: the Statisticians, the Accountants, the lesser breeds and the higher. He hated them because they owned their smug knowledge now, knew their fate, while he himself, empty still, had to face some kind of further red tape.

He reached 15-C, was ushered in and left in an empty room. For one moment, his spirits bounded. Surely, if this were the Labour classification room, there would be dozens of youngsters present.

A door sucked into its recess on the other side of a waist-high partition and an elderly, white-haired man stepped out. He smiled and showed even teeth that were obviously false, but his face was still ruddy and his voice had vigour.

He said, 'Good evening, George. Our own sector has only one of you this time, I see.'

'Only one?' said George blankly.

'Thousands over the Earth, of course. Thousands. You're not alone.'

George felt exasperated. He said, 'I don't understand, sir. What's my classification? What's happening?'

'Easy, son. You're all right. It could happen to anyone.' He held out his hand and George took it mechanically. It was warm and it pressed George's hand firmly. 'Sit down, son. I'm Sam Ellenford.'

George nodded impatiently. 'I want to know what's going on, sir.'

'Of course. To begin with, you can't be a Computer Programmer, George. You've guessed that, I think.'

'Yes, I have,' said George bitterly. 'What will I be, then?'

'That's the hard part to explain, George.' He paused, then said with careful distinctness, 'Nothing.'

'*What!*'

'Nothing!'

'But what does that mean? Why can't you assign me a profession?'

'We have no choice in the matter, George. It's the structure of your mind that decides that.'

George went a sallow yellow. His eyes bulged. 'There's something wrong with my mind?'

'There's *something* about it. As far as professional classification is concerned, I suppose you can call it wrong.'

'But why?'

Ellenford shrugged. 'I'm sure you know how Earth runs its Educational programme, George. Practically any human being can absorb practically any body of knowledge, but each individual brain pattern is better suited to receiving some types of knowledge than others. We try to match mind to knowledge as well as we can within the limits of the quota requirements for each profession.'

George nodded. 'Yes, I know.'

'Every once in a while, George, we come up against a young man whose mind is not suited to receiving a superimposed knowledge of any sort.'

'You mean I can't be Educated?'

'That is what I mean.'

'But that's crazy. I'm intelligent. I can understand – ' He looked helplessly about as though trying to find some way of proving that he had a functioning brain.

'Don't misunderstand me, please,' said Ellenford gravely. 'You're intelligent. There's no question about that. You're even above average in intelligence. Unfortunately that has nothing to do with whether the mind ought to be allowed to accept superimposed knowledge or not. In fact, it is almost always the intelligent person who comes here.'

'You mean I can't even be a Registered Labourer?' babbled George. Suddenly even that was better than the blank that faced him. 'What's there to know to be a Labourer?'

'Don't underestimate the Labourer, young man. There are dozens of subclassifications and each variety has its own corpus of fairly detailed knowledge. Do you think there's no skill in knowing the proper manner of lifting a weight? Besides, for the Labourer, we must select not only minds suited to it, but bodies as well. You're not the type, George, to last long as a Labourer.'

George was conscious of his slight build. He said, 'But I've never heard of anyone without a profession.'

'There aren't many,' conceded Ellenford. 'And we protect them.'

'Protect them?' George felt confusion and fright grow higher inside him.

'You're a ward of the planet, George. From the time you walked through that door, we've been in charge of you.' And he smiled.

It was a fond smile. To George it seemed the smile of ownership; the smile of a grown man for a helpless child.

He said, 'You mean, I'm going to be in prison?'

'Of course not. You will simply be with others of your kind.'

Your kind. The words made a kind of thunder in George's ear.

Ellenford said, 'You need special treatment. We'll take care of you.'

To George's own horror, he burst into tears. Ellenford walked to the other end of the room and faced away as though in thought.

George fought to reduce the agonized weeping to sobs and then to strangle those. He thought of his father and mother, of his friends, of Trevelyan, of his own shame --

He said rebelliously, 'I learned to read.'

'Everyone with a whole mind can do that. We've never found exceptions. It is at this stage that we discover – exceptions. And when you learned to read, George, we were concerned about your mind pattern. Certain peculiarities were reported even then by the doctor in charge.'

'Can't you try Educating me? You haven't even tried. I'm willing to take the risk.'

'The law forbids us to do that, George. But look, it will not be bad. We will explain matters to your family so they will not be hurt. At the place to which you'll be taken, you'll be allowed privileges. We'll get you books and you can learn what you will.'

'Dab knowledge in by hand,' said George bitterly. 'Shred by shred. Then, when I die I'll know enough to be a Registered Junior Office Boy, Paper-Clip Division.'

'Yet I understand you've already been studying books.'

George froze. He was struck devastatingly by sudden understanding. 'That's it . . .'

'What is?'

'That fellow Antonelli. He's knifing me.'

'No, George. You're quite wrong.'

'Don't tell me that.' George was in an ecstasy of fury. 'That lousy bastard is selling me out because he thought I was a little too wise for him. I read books and tried to get a head start towards programming. Well, what do you want to square things? Money? You won't get it. I'm getting out of here and when I finish broadcasting this – '

He was screaming.

Ellenford shook his head and touched a contact.

Two men entered on catfeet and got on either side of George. They pinned his arms to his sides. One of them used an air-spray hypodermic in the hollow of his right elbow and the hypnotic entered his vein and had an almost immediate effect.

His screams cut off and his head fell forward. His knees buckled and only the men on either side kept him erect as he slept.

They took care of George as they said they would; they were good to him and unfailingly kind – about the way,

George thought, he himself would be to a sick kitten he had taken pity on.

They told him that he should sit up and take some interest in life; and then told him that most people who came here had the same attitude of despair at the beginning and that he would snap out of it.

He didn't even hear them.

Dr Ellenford himself visited him to tell him that his parents had been informed that he was away on special assignment.

George muttered, 'Do they know – '

Ellenford assured him at once, 'We gave no details.'

At first George had refused to eat. They fed him intravenously. They hid sharp objects and kept him under guard. Hali Omani came to be his room-mate and his stolidity had a calming effect.

One day, out of sheer desperate boredom, George asked for a book. Omani, who himself read books constantly, looked up, smiling broadly. George almost withdrew the request then, rather than give any of them satisfaction, then thought: What do I care?

He didn't specify the book and Omani brought one on chemistry. It was in big print, with small words and many illustrations. It was for teenagers. He threw the book violently against the wall.

That's what he would be always. A teenager all his life. A pre-Educate forever and special books would have to be written for him. He lay smouldering in bed, staring at the ceiling, and after an hour had passed, he got up sulkily, picked up the book, and began reading.

It took him a week to finish it and then he asked for another.

'Do you want me to take the first one back?' asked Omani. George frowned. There were things in the book he had not understood, yet he was not so lost to shame as to say so.

But Omani said, 'Come to think of it, you'd better keep it. Books are meant to be read and re-read.'

It was that same day that he finally yielded to Omani's invitation that he tour the place. He dogged at the Nigerian's feet and took in his surroundings with quick hostile glances.

The place was no prison certainly. There were no walls, no

locked doors, no guards. But it was a prison in that the inmates had no place to go outside.

It was somehow good to see others like himself by the dozen. It was so easy to believe himself to be the only one in the world so – maimed.

He mumbled, 'How many people here anyway?'

'Two hundred and five, George, and this isn't the only place of the sort in the world. There are thousands.'

Men looked up as he passed, wherever he went; in the gymnasium, along the tennis courts; through the library (he had never in his life imagined books could exist in such numbers; they were stacked, actually stacked, along long shelves). They stared at him curiously and he returned the looks savagely. At least *they* were no better than he; no call for *them* to look at him as though he were some sort of curiosity.

Most of them were in their twenties. George said suddenly, 'What happens to the older ones?'

Omani said, 'This place specializes in the younger ones.' Then, as though he suddenly recognized an implication in George's question that he had missed earlier, he shook his head gravely and said, 'They're not put out of the way, if that's what you mean. There are other Houses for older ones.'

'Who cares?' mumbled George, who felt he was sounding too interested and in danger of slipping into surrender.

'You might. As you grow older, you will find yourself in a House with occupants of both sexes.'

That surprised George somehow. 'Women, too?'

'Of course. Do you suppose women are immune to this sort of thing?'

George thought of that with more interest and excitement than he had felt for anything since before that day when – He forced his thought away from that.

Omani stopped at the doorway of a room that contained a small closed-circuit television set and a desk computer. Five or six men sat about the television. Omani said, 'This is a classroom.'

George said, 'What's that?'

'The young men in there are being educated. Not,' he added, quickly, 'in the usual way.'

'You mean they're cramming it in bit by bit.'

'That's right. This is the way everyone did it in ancient times.'

This was what they kept telling him since he had come to the House but what of it? Suppose there had been a day when mankind had not known the diatherm-oven. Did that mean he should be satisfied to eat meat raw in a world where others ate it cooked?

He said, 'Why do they want to go through that bit-by-bit stuff?'

'To pass the time, George, and because they're curious.'

'What good does it do them?'

'It makes them happier.'

George carried that thought to bed with him.

The next day he said to Omani ungraciously, 'Can you get me into a classroom where I can find out something about programming?'

Omani replied heartily, 'Sure.'

It was slow and he resented it. Why should someone have to explain something and explain it again? Why should he have to read and re-read a passage, then stare at a mathematical relationship and not understand it at once? That wasn't how other people had to be.

Over and over again, he gave up. Once he refused to attend classes for a week.

But always he returned. The official in charge, who assigned reading, conducted the television demonstrations, and even explained difficult passages and concepts, never commented on the matter.

George was finally given a regular task in the gardens and took his turn in the various kitchen and cleaning details. This was represented to him as being an advance, but he wasn't fooled. The place might have been far more mechanized than it was, but they deliberately made work for the young men in order to give them the illusion of worthwhile occupation, of usefulness. George wasn't fooled.

They were even paid small sums of money out of which they could buy certain specified luxuries or which they could put aside for a problematical use in a problematical old age. George kept his money in an open jar, which he kept on a closet shelf. He had no idea how much he had accumulated. Nor did he care.

He made no real friends though he reached the stage where a civil good day was in order. He even stopped brooding (or almost stopped) on the miscarriage of justice that had placed him there. He would go weeks without dreaming of Antonelli, of his gross nose and wattled neck, of the leer with which he would push George into a boiling quicksand and hold him under, till he woke screaming with Omani bending over him in concern.

Omani said to him on a snowy day in February, 'It's amazing how you're adjusting.'

But that was February, the thirteenth to be exact, his nineteenth birthday. March came, then April, and with the approach of May he realized he hadn't adjusted at all.

The previous May had passed unregarded while George was still in his bed, drooping and ambitionless. This May was different.

All over Earth, George knew, Olympics would be taking place and young men would be competing, matching their skills against one another in the fight for a place on a new world. There would be the holiday atmosphere, the excitement, the news reports, the self-contained recruiting agents from the worlds beyond space, the glory of victory or the consolations of defeat.

How much of fiction dealt with these motifs; how much of his own boyhood excitement lay in following the events of Olympics from year to year; how many of his own plans –

George Platen could not conceal the longing in his voice. It was too much to suppress. He said, 'Tomorrow's the first of May. Olympics!'

And that led to his first quarrel with Omani and to Omani's bitter enunciation of the exact name of the institution in which George found himself.

Omani gazed fixedly at George and said distinctly, 'A House for the Feeble-minded.'

George Platen flushed. Feeble-minded!

He rejected it desperately. He said in a monotone, 'I'm leaving.' He said it on impulse. His conscious mind learned it first from the statement as he uttered it.

Omani, who had returned to his book, looked up. 'What?'

George knew what he was saying now. He said it fiercely, 'I'm leaving.'

'That's ridiculous. Sit down, George, calm yourself.'

'Oh, no. I'm here on a frame-up, I tell you. This doctor, Antonelli, took a dislike to me. It's the sense of power these petty bureaucrats have. Cross them and they wipe out your life with a stylus mark on some card file.'

'Are you back to that?'

'And staying there till it's all straightened out. I'm going to get to Antonelli somehow, break him, force the truth out of him.' George was breathing heavily and he felt feverish. Olympics month was here and he couldn't let it pass. If he did, it would be the final surrender and he would be lost for all time.

Omani threw his legs over the side of his bed and stood up. He was nearly six feet tall and the expression on his face gave him the look of a concerned Saint Bernard. He put his arm about George's shoulder. 'If I hurt your feeling – '

George shrugged him off. 'You just said what you thought was the truth, and I'm going to prove it isn't the truth, that's all. Why not? The door's open. There aren't any locks. No one ever said I couldn't leave. I'll just walk out.'

'All right, but where will you go?'

'To the nearest air terminal, then to the nearest Olympics centre. I've got money.' He seized the open jar that held the wages he had put away. Some of the coins jangled to the floor.

'That will last you a week maybe. Then what?'

'By then I'll have things settled.'

'By then you'll come crawling back here,' said Omani earnestly, 'with all the progress you've made to do over again. You're mad, George.'

'Feeble-minded is the word you used before.'

'Well, I'm sorry I did. Stay here, will you?'

'Are you going to try to stop me?'

Omani compressed his full lips. 'No, I guess I won't. This is your business. If the only way you can learn is to buck the world and come back with blood on your face, go ahead. – Well, go ahead.'

George was in the doorway now, looking back over his shoulder. 'I'm going,' – he came back to pick up his pocket grooming set slowly – 'I hope you don't object to me taking a few personal belongings.'

Omani shrugged. He was in bed again reading, indifferent.

George lingered at the door again, but Omani didn't look up. George gritted his teeth, turned and walked rapidly down the empty corridor and out into the night-shrouded grounds.

He had expected to be stopped before leaving the grounds. He wasn't. He had stopped at an all-night diner to ask directions to an air terminal and expected the proprietor to call the police. That didn't happen. He summoned a skimmer to take him to the airport and the driver asked no questions.

Yet he felt no lift at that. He arrived at the airport sick at heart. He had not realized how the outer world would be. He was surrounded by professionals. The diner's proprietor had had his name inscribed on the plastic shell over the cash register. So and so, Registered Cook. The man in the skimmer had his licence up, Registered Chauffeur. George felt the bareness of his name and experienced a kind of nakedness because of it; worse, he felt skinned. But no one challenged him. No one studied him suspiciously and demanded proof of professional rating.

George thought bitterly: Who would imagine any human being without one?

He bought a ticket to San Francisco on the 3 a.m. plane. No other plane for a sizeable Olympics centre was leaving before morning and he wanted to wait as little as possible. As it was, he sat huddled in the waiting room, watching for the police. They did not come.

He was in San Francisco before noon and the noise of the city struck him like a blow. This was the largest city he had ever seen and he had been used to silence and calm for a year and a half now.

Worse, it was Olympics month. He almost forgot his own predicament in his sudden awareness that some of the noise, excitement, confusion was due to that.

The Olympics boards were up at the airport for the benefit of the incoming travellers, and crowds jostled around each one. Each major profession had its own board. Each listed directions to the Olympics Hall where the contest for that day for that profession would be given; the individuals competing and their city of birth; the Outworld (if any) sponsoring it.

It was a completely stylized thing. George had read descriptions often enough in the newsprints and films, watched matches on television, and even witnessed a small Olympics in the Registered Butcher classification at the county seat. Even that, which had no conceivable Galactic implication (there was no Outworlder in attendance, of course) aroused excitement enough.

Partly, the excitement was caused simply by the fact of competition, partly by the spur of local pride (oh, when there was a home-town boy to cheer for, though he might be a complete stranger), and, of course, partly by betting. There was no way of stopping the last.

George found it difficult to approach the board. He found himself looking at the scurrying, avid onlookers in a new way.

There must have been a time when they themselves were Olympic material. What had *they* done? Nothing!

If they had been winners, they would be far out in the Galaxy somewhere, not stuck here on Earth. Whatever they were, their professions must have made them Earth-bait from the beginning; or else they had made themselves Earth-bait by inefficiency at whatever high-specialized professions they had had.

Now these failures stood about and speculated on the chances of newer and younger men. Vultures!

How he wished they were speculating on him.

He moved down the line of boards blankly, clinging to the outskirts of the groups about them. He had eaten breakfast on the strato and he wasn't hungry. He was afraid, though. He was in a big city during the confusion of the beginning of Olympics competition. That was protection, sure. The city was full of strangers. No one would question George. No one would care about George.

No one would care. Not even the House, thought George bitterly. They cared for him like a sick kitten, but if a sick kitten ups and wanders off, well, too bad, what can you do?

And now that he was in San Francisco, what did he do?

His thoughts struck blankly against a wall. See someone? Whom? How? Where would he even stay? The money he had left seemed pitiful.

The first shamefaced thought of going back came to him. He could go to the police – He shook his head violently as though arguing with a material adversary.

A word caught his eye on one of the boards, gleaming there: *Metallurgist*. In smaller letters, *non-ferrous*. At the bottom of a long list of names, in flowing script, *sponsored by Novia*.

It induced painful memories: himself arguing with Trevelyan, so certain that he himself would be a Programmer, so certain that a Programmer was superior to a Metallurgist, so certain that he was following the right course, so certain that he was clever –

So clever that he had to boast to that small-minded, vindictive Antonelli. He had been so sure of himself that moment when he had been called and had left the nervous Trevelyan standing there, so cocksure.

George cried out in a short, incoherent high-pitched gasp. Someone turned to look at him, then hurried on. People brushed past impatiently pushing him this way and that. He remained staring at the board, open-mouthed.

It was as though the board had answered his thought. He was thinking 'Trevelyan' so hard that it had seemed for a moment that of course the board would say 'Trevelyan' back at him.

But that *was* Trevelyan, up there. And *Armand* Trevelyan (Stubby's hated first name; up in lights for everyone to see) and the right hometown. What's more, Trev had wanted Novia, aimed for Novia, insisted on Novia; and this competition was sponsored by Novia.

This had to be Trev; good old Trev. Almost without thinking, he noted the directions for getting to the place of competition and took his place in line for a skimmer.

Then he thought sombrely: Trev made it! He wanted to be a Metallurgist, and he made it!

George felt colder, more alone than ever.

There was a line waiting to enter the hall. Apparently, Metallurgy Olympics was to be an exciting and closely fought one. At least, the illuminated sky sign above the hall said so, and the jostling crowd seemed to think so.

It would have been a rainy day, George thought, from the colour of the sky, but San Francisco had drawn the shield across its breadth from bay to ocean. It was an expense to do so, of course, but all expenses were warranted where the comfort of Outworlders was concerned. They would be in town for the Olympics. They were heavy spenders. And for each recruit taken, there would be a fee both to Earth and to the local government from the planet sponsoring the Olympics. It paid to keep Outworlders in mind of a particular city as a pleasant place in which to spend Olympics time. San Francisco knew what it was doing.

George, lost in thought, was suddenly aware of a gentle pressure on his shoulder blade and a voice saying, 'Are you in line here, young man?'

The line had moved up without George's having noticed the widening gap. He stepped forward hastily and muttered, 'Sorry, sir.'

There was the touch of two fingers on the elbow of his jacket and he looked about furtively.

The man behind him nodded cheerfully. He had iron-grey hair, and under his jacket he wore an old-fashioned sweater that buttoned down the front. He said, 'I didn't mean to sound sarcastic.'

'No offence.'

'All right, then.' He sounded cosily talkative. 'I wasn't sure you might not simply be standing there, entangled with the line, so to speak, only by accident. I thought you might be a –'

'A what?' said George sharply.

'Why, a contestant, of course. You look young.'

George turned away. He felt neither cosy nor talkative, and bitterly impatient with busybodies.

A thought struck him. Had an alarm been sent out for him? Was his description known, or his picture? Was Greyhair behind him trying to get a good look at his face?

He hadn't seen any news reports. He craned his neck to see the moving strips of news headlines parading across one section of the city shield, somewhat lack-lustre against the grey of the cloudy afternoon sky. It was no use. He gave up at once. The headlines would never concern themselves with him. This was Olympics time and the only news worth head-lining was the comparative scores of the winners and the trophies won by continents, nations, and cities.

It would go on like that for weeks, with scores calculated on a per capita basis and every city finding some way of calculating itself into a position of honour. His own town had once placed third in an Olympics covering Wiring Technician; third in the whole state. There was still a plaque saying so in Town Hall.

George hunched his head between his shoulders and shoved his hands in his pockets and decided that made him more noticeable. He relaxed and tried to look unconcerned, and felt no safer. He was in the lobby now, and no authoritative hand had yet been laid on his shoulder. He filed into the hall itself and moved as far forward as he could.

It was with an unpleasant shock that he noticed Greyhair next to him. He looked away quickly and tried reasoning with himself. The man had been right behind him in line after all.

Greyhair, beyond a brief and tentative smile, paid no attention to him and, besides, the Olympics was about to start. George rose in his seat to see if he could make out the position assigned to Trevelyan and at the moment that was all his concern.

The hall was moderate in size and shaped in the classical long oval, with the spectators in the two balconies running completely about the rim and the contestants in the linear trough down the centre. The machines were set up, the progress boards above each bench were dark, except for the name and contest number of each man. The contestants themselves were on the scene, reading, talking together; one was checking his fingernails minutely. (It was, of course, considered bad form for any contestant to pay any attention to the problem before him until the instant of the starting signal.)

George studied the programme sheet he found in the appropriate slot in the arm of his chair and found Trevelyan's name. His number was twelve and, to George's chagrin, that was at the wrong end of the hall. He could make out the figure of Contestant Twelve, standing with his hands in his pockets, back to his machine, and staring at the audience as though he were counting the house. George couldn't make out the face.

Still, that was Trev.

George sank back in his seat. He wondered if Trev would do well. He hoped, as a matter of conscious duty, that he would, and yet there was something within him that felt rebelliously resentful. George, professionless, here, watching. Trevelyan, Registered Metallurgist, Non-ferrous, there, competing.

George wondered if Trevelyan had competed in his first year. Sometimes men did, if they felt particularly confident – or hurried. It involved a certain risk. However efficient the Educative process, a preliminary year on Earth ('oiling the stiff knowledge', as the expression went) ensured a higher score.

If Trevelyan was repeating, maybe he wasn't doing so well. George felt ashamed that the thought pleased him just a bit.

He looked about. The stands were almost full. This would be a well-attended Olympics, which meant greater strain on the contestants – or greater drive, perhaps, depending on the individual.

Why Olympics, he thought suddenly? He had never known. Why was bread called bread?

Once he had asked his father: 'Why do they call it Olympics, Dad?'

And his father had said: 'Olympics means competition.'

George had said: 'Is when Stubby and I fight an Olympics, Dad?'

Platen, Senior, had said: 'No. Olympics is a special kind of competition and don't ask silly questions. You'll know all you have to know when you get Educated.'

George, back in the present, sighed and crowded down into his seat.

All you have to know!

Funny that the memory should be so clear now. 'When you get Educated.' No one ever said, '*If* you get Educated.'

He always had asked silly questions, it seemed to him now. It was as though his mind had some instinctive foreknowledge of its inability to be Educated and had gone about asking questions in order to pick up scraps here and there as best it could.

And at the House they encouraged him to do so because they agreed with his mind's instinct. It was the only way.

He sat up suddenly. What the devil was he doing? Falling for that lie? Was it because Trev was there before him, an Educee, competing in the Olympics that he himself was surrendering?

He *wasn't* feeble-minded! *No!*

And the shout of denial in his mind was echoed by the sudden clamour in the audience as everyone got to his feet.

The box seat in the very centre of one long side of the oval was filling with an entourage wearing the colours of Novia, and the word 'Novia' went up above them on the main board.

Novia was a Grade A world with a large population and a thoroughly developed civilization, perhaps the best in the Galaxy. It was the kind of world that every Earthman wanted to live in someday; or, failing that, to see his children live in. (George remembered Trevelyan's insistence on Novia as a goal – and there he was competing for it.)

The lights went out in that section of the ceiling above the audience and so did the wall lights. The central trough, in which the contestants waited, became floodlit.

Again George tried to make out Trevelyan. Too far.

The clear, polished voice of the announcer sounded. 'Distinguished Novian sponsors. Ladies. Gentlemen. The Olympics competition for Metallurgist, Non-ferrous, is about to begin. The contestants are – '

Carefully and conscientiously, he read off the list in the programme. Names. Home towns. Educative years. Each name received its cheers, the San Franciscans among them receiving the loudest. When Trevelyan's name was reached, George surprised himself by shouting and waving madly. The grey-haired man next to him surprised him even more by cheering likewise.

George could not help but stare in astonishment and his neighbour leaned over to say (speaking loudly in order to be heard over the hubbub), 'No one here from my home town; I'll root for yours. Someone you know?'

George shrank back. 'No.'

'I noticed you looking in that direction. Would you like to borrow my glasses?'

'No. Thank you.' (Why didn't the old fool mind his own business?)

The announcer went on with other formal details concerning the serial number of the competition, the method of timing and scoring and so on. Finally, he approached the meat of the matter and the audience grew silent as it listened.

'Each contestant will be supplied with a bar of non-ferrous alloy of unspecified composition. He will be required to sample and assay the bar, reporting all results correctly to four decimals in per cent. All will utilize for this purpose a Beeman Microspectrograph, Model FX-2, each of which is, at the moment, not in working order.'

There was an appreciative shout from the audience.

'Each contestant will be required to analyse the fault of his machine and correct it. Tools and spare parts are supplied. The spare part necessary may not be present, in which case it must be asked for, and time of delivery thereof will be deducted from final time. Are all contestants ready?'

The board above Contestant Five flashed a frantic red signal. Contestant Five ran off the floor and returned a moment later. The audience laughed good-naturedly.

'Are all contestants ready?'

The boards remained blank.

'Any questions?'

Still blank.

'You may begin.'

There was, of course, no way anyone in the audience could tell how any contestant was progressing except for whatever notations went up on the notice board. But then, that didn't matter. Except for what professional Metallurgists there might be in the audience, none would understand anything about the contest professionally in any case. What was important was who won, who was second, who was third. For those who had bets on the standings (illegal, but unpreventable) that was all-important. Everything else might go hang.

George watched as eagerly as the rest, glancing from one contestant to the next, observing how this one had removed the cover from his microspectrograph with deft strokes of a small instrument; how that one was peering into the face of the thing; how still a third was setting his alloy bar in its holder; and how a fourth adjusted a vernier with such small touches that he seemed momentarily frozen.

Trevelyan was as absorbed as the rest. George had no way of telling how he was doing.

The notice board over Contestant Seventeen flashed: Focus plate out of adjustment.

The audience cheered wildly.

Contestant Seventeen might be right and he might, of course, be wrong. If the latter, he would have to correct his diagnosis later and lose time. Or he might never correct his diagnosis and be unable to complete his analysis or, worse still, end with a completely wrong analysis.

Never mind. For the moment, the audience cheered.

Other boards lit up. George watched for Board Twelve. That came on finally: Sample holder off-centre. New clamp depresser needed.

An attendant went running to him with a new part. If Trevelyan was wrong, it would mean useless delay. Nor would the time elapsed in waiting for the part be deducted. George found himself holding his breath.

Results were beginning to go up on Board Seventeen, in gleaming letters: aluminium, 41.2649; magnesium, 22.1914; copper, 10.1001.

Here and there, other boards began sprouting figures.

The audience was in bedlam.

George wondered how the contestants could work in such pandemonium, then wondered if that were not even a good thing. A first-class technician should work best under pressure.

Seventeen rose from his place as his board went red-rimmed to signify completion. Four was only two seconds behind him. Another, then another.

Trevelyan was still working, the minor constituents of his alloy bar still unreported. With nearly all contestants standing, Trevelyan finally rose, also. Then, tailing off, Five rose, and received an ironic cheer.

It wasn't over. Official announcements were naturally delayed. Time elapsed was something, but accuracy was just as important. And not all diagnoses were of equal difficulty. A dozen factors had to be weighed.

Finally, the announcer's voice sounded, 'Winner in the time of four minutes and twelve seconds, diagnosis correct, analysis correct within an average of zero point seven parts per hundred thousand, Contestant Number – *Seventeen*, Henry Anton Schmidt of – '

What followed was drowned in the screaming. Number Eight was next and then Four, whose good time was spoiled by a five part in ten thousand error in the niobium figure. Twelve was never mentioned. He was an also-ran.

George made his way through the crowd to the Contestants' Door and found a large clot of humanity ahead of him. There would be weeping relatives (joy or sorrow, depending) to greet them, newsmen to interview the topscorers, or the home-town boys, autograph hounds, publicity seekers and the just plain curious. Girls, too, who might hope to catch the eye of a top-scorer, almost certainly headed for Novia (or perhaps a low-scorer who needed consolation and had the cash to afford it).

George hung back. He saw no one he knew. With San Francisco so far from home, it seemed pretty safe to assume that there would be no relatives to condole with Trev on the spot.

Contestants emerged, smiling weakly, nodding at shouts of approval. Policemen kept the crowds far enough away to allow a lane for walking. Each high-scorer drew a portion of the crowd off with him, like a magnet pushing through a mound of iron filings.

When Trevelyan walked out, scarcely anyone was left. (George felt somehow that he had delayed coming out until just that had come to pass.) There was a cigarette in his dour mouth and he turned, eyes downcast, to walk off.

It was the first hint of home George had had in what was almost a year and a half and seemed almost a decade and a half. He was almost amazed that Trevelyan hadn't aged, that he was the same Trev he had last seen.

George sprang forward. '*Trev!*'

Trevelyan spun about, astonished. He stared at George and then his hand shot out. 'George Platen, *what* the devil – '

And almost as soon as the look of pleasure had crossed his face, it left. His hand dropped before George had quite the chance of seizing it.

'Were you in there?' A curt jerk of Trev's head indicated the hall.

'I was.'

'To see me?'

'Yes.'

'Didn't do so well, did I?' He dropped his cigarette and stepped on it, staring off to the street, where the emerging crowd was slowly eddying and finding its way into skimmers, while new lines were forming for the next scheduled Olympics.

Trevelyan said heavily, 'So what? It's only the second time I missed. Novia can go shove after the deal I got today. There are planets that would jump at me fast enough – But, listen, I haven't seen you since Education Day. Where did you go? Your folks said you were on special assignment but gave no details and you never wrote. You might have written.'

'I should have,' said George uneasily. 'Anyway, I came to say I was sorry the way things went just now.'

'Don't be,' said Trevelyan. 'I told you. Novia can go shove – At that I should have known. They've been saying for weeks that the Beeman machine would be used. All the wise money was on Beeman machines. The damned Education tapes they ran through me were for Henslers and who uses Henslers? The worlds in the Goman Cluster if you want to call them worlds. Wasn't *that* a nice deal they gave me?'

'Can't you complain to – '

'Don't be a fool. They'll tell me my brain was built for Henslers. Go argue. *Everything* went wrong. I was the only one who had to send out for a piece of equipment. Notice that?'

'They deducted the time for that, though.'

'Sure, but I lost time wondering if I could be right in my diagnosis when I noticed there wasn't any clamp depresser in the parts they had supplied. They don't deduct for that. If it had been a Hensler, I would have *known* I was right. How could I match up then? The top winner was a San Franciscan. So were three of the next four. And the fifth guy was from Los Angeles. They get big-city Educational tapes. The best available. Beeman spectrographs and all. How do I compete with them? I came all the way out here just to get a chance at a Novian-sponsored Olympics in my classification and I might just as well have stayed home. I knew it, I tell you, and that settles it. Novia isn't the only chunk of rock in space.

Of all the damned – '

He wasn't speaking to George. He wasn't speaking to anyone. He was just uncorked and frothing. George realized that.

George said, 'If you knew in advance that the Beemans were going to be used, couldn't you have studied up on them ?'

'They weren't in my tapes, I tell you.'

'You could have read – books.'

The last two words had tailed off under Trevelyan's suddenly sharp look.

Trevelyan said, 'Are you trying to make a big laugh out of this ? You think this is funny ? How do you expect me to read some book and try to memorize enough to match someone else who *knows*?'

'I thought – '

'You try it. You try – ' Then, suddenly, 'What's your profession, by the way ?' He sounded thoroughly hostile.

'Well – '

'Come on, now. If you're going to be a wise guy with me, let's see what you've done. You're still on Earth, I notice, so you're not a Computer Programmer and your special assignment can't be much.'

George said, 'Listen, Trev, I'm late for an appointment.' He backed away, trying to smile.

'No, you don't.' Trevelyan reached out fiercely, catching hold of George's jacket. 'You answer my question. Why are you afraid to tell me? What is it with you? Don't come here rubbing a bad showing in my face, George, unless you can take it, too. Do you hear me ?'

He was shaking George in frenzy and they were struggling and swaying across the floor, when the Voice of Doom struck George's ear in the form of a policeman's outraged call.

'All right now. *All* right. Break it up.'

George's heart turned to lead and lurched sickeningly. The policeman would be taking names, asking to see identity cards, and George lacked one. He would be questioned and his lack of profession would show at once; and before Trevelyan, too, who ached with the pain of the drubbing he had taken and would spread the news back home as a salve for his own hurt feelings.

George couldn't stand that. He broke away from Trevelyan and made to run, but the policeman's heavy hand was on his shoulder. 'Hold on, there. Let's see your identity card.'

Trevelyan was fumbling for his, saying harshly, 'I'm Armand Trevelyan, Metallurgist, Non-ferrous. I was just competing in the Olympics. You better find out about him, though, officer.'

George faced the two, lips dry and throat thickened past speech.

Another voice sounded, quiet, well-mannered. 'Officer. One moment.'

The policeman stepped back. 'Yes, sir?'

'This young man is my guest. What is the trouble?'

George looked about in wild surprise. It was the grey-haired man who had been sitting next to him. Greyhair nodded benignly at George.

Guest? Was he mad?

The policeman was saying, 'These two were creating a disturbance, sir.'

'Any criminal charges? Any damages?'

'No, sir.'

'Well, then, I'll be responsible.' He presented a small card to the policeman's view and the latter stepped back at once.

Trevelyan began indignantly, 'Hold on, now – ' but the policeman turned on him.

'All right, now. Got any charges?'

'I just – '

'On your way. The rest of you – move on.' A sizeable crowd had gathered, which now, reluctantly, unknotted itself and travelled away.

George let himself be led to a skimmer but baulked at entering.

He said, 'Thank you, but I'm not your guest.' (Could it be a ridiculous case of mistaken identity?)

But Greyhair smiled and said, 'You weren't but you are now. Let me introduce myself, I'm Ladislas Ingenescu, Registered Historian.'

'But – '

'Come, you will come to no harm, I assure you. After all, I only wanted to spare you some trouble with a policeman.'

'But why?'

'Do you want a reason? Well, then, say that we're honorary towns-mates, you and I. We both shouted for the same man, remember, and we townspeople must stick together, even if the tie is only honorary. Eh?'

And George, completely unsure of this man, Ingenescu, and of himself as well, found himself inside the skimmer. Before he could make up his mind that he ought to get off again, they were off the ground.

He thought confusedly: The man has some status. The policeman deferred to him.

He was almost forgetting that his real purpose here in San Francisco was not to find Trevelyan but to find some person with enough influence to force a reappraisal of his own capacity of Education.

It could be that Ingenescu was such a man. And right in George's lap.

Everything could be working out fine – fine. Yet it sounded hollow in his thought. He was uneasy.

During the short skimmer-hop, Ingenescu kept up an even flow of small-talk, pointing out the landmarks of the city, reminiscing about past Olympics he had seen. George, who paid just enough attention to make vague sounds during the pauses, watched the route of flight anxiously.

Would they head for one of the shield-openings and leave the city altogether?

No, they headed downward, and George sighed his relief softly. He felt safer in the city.

The skimmer landed at the roof-entry of a hotel and, as he alighted, Ingenescu said, 'I hope you'll eat dinner with me in my room?'

George said, 'Yes', and grinned unaffectedly. He was just beginning to realize the gap left within him by a missing lunch.

Ingenescu let George eat in silence. Night closed in and the wall lights went on automatically. (George thought: I've been on my own almost twenty-four hours.)

And then over the coffee, Ingenescu finally spoke again. He said, 'You've been acting as though you think I intend you harm.'

George reddened, put down his cup and tried to deny it, but the older man laughed and shook his head.

'It's so. I've been watching you closely since I first saw you and I think I know a great deal about you now.'

George half rose in horror.

Ingenescu said, 'But sit down. I only want to help you.'

George sat down but his thoughts were in a whirl. If the old man knew who he was, why had he not left him to the policeman? On the other hand, why should he volunteer help?

Ingenescu said, 'You want to know why I should want to help you? Oh, don't look alarmed. I can't read minds. It's just that my training enables me to judge the little reactions that give minds away, you see. Do you understand that?'

George shook his head.

Ingenescu said, 'Consider my first sight of you. You were waiting in line to watch an Olympics, and your micro-reactions didn't match what you were doing. The expression of your face was wrong, the action of your hands was wrong. It meant that something, in general, was wrong, and the interesting thing was that, whatever it was, it was nothing common, nothing obvious. Perhaps, I thought, it was something of which your own conscious mind was unaware.

'I couldn't help but follow you, sit next to you. I followed you again when you left and eavesdropped on the conversation between your friend and yourself. After that, well, you were far too interesting an object of study – I'm sorry if that sounds cold-blooded – for me to allow you to be taken off by a policeman. – Now tell me, what is it that troubles you?'

George was in an agony of indecision. If this was a trap, why should it be such an indirect, roundabout one? And he *had* to turn to someone. He had come to the city to find help and here was help being offered. Perhaps what was wrong was that it was being offered. It came too easy.

Ingenescu said, 'Of course, what you tell me as a Social Scientist is a privileged communication. Do you know what that means?'

'No, sir.'

'It means, it would be dishonourable for me to repeat what you say to anyone for any purpose. Moreover no one has the legal right to compel me to repeat it.'

George said, with sudden suspicion, 'I thought you were a Historian.'

'So I am.'

'Just now you said you were a Social Scientist.'

Ingenescu broke into loud laughter and apologized for it when he could talk. 'I'm sorry, young man, I shouldn't laugh, and I wasn't really laughing at you. I was laughing at Earth and its emphasis on physical science, and the practical segments of it at that. I'll bet you can rattle off every subdivision of construction technology or mechanical engineering and yet you're a blank on social science.'

'Well, then, what *is* social science?'

'Social science studies groups of human beings and there are many highly specialized branches to it, just as there are to zoology, for instance. For instance, there are Culturists, who study the mechanics of cultures, their growth, development, and decay. Cultures,' he added, forestalling a question, 'are all the aspects of a way of life. For instance it includes the way we make our living, the things we enjoy and believe, what we consider good and bad and so on. Do you understand?'

'I think I do.'

'An Economist – not an Economic Statistician, now, but an Economist – specializes in the study of the way a culture supplies the bodily needs of its individual members. A Psychologist specializes in the individual member of a society and how he is affected by the society. A Futurist specializes in planning the future course of a society, and a Historian – That's where I come in, now.'

'Yes, sir.'

'A Historian specializes in the past development of our own society and of societies with other cultures.'

George found himself interested. 'Was it different in the past?'

'I should say it was. Until a thousand years ago, there was no Education; not what we call Education, at least.'

George said, 'I know. People learned in bits and pieces out of books.'

'Why, how do you know this?'

'I've heard it said,' said George cautiously. Then, 'Is there

145

any use in worrying about what's happened long ago? I mean, it's all done with, isn't it?'

'It's never done with, my boy. The past explains the present. For instance, why is our Educational system what it is?'

George stirred restlessly. The man kept bringing the subject back to that. He said snappishly, 'Because it's best.'

'Ah, but why is it best? Now you listen to me for one moment and I'll explain. Then you can tell me if there is any use in history. Even before interstellar travel was developed –' He broke off at the look of complete astonishment on George's face. 'Well, did you think we always had it?'

'I never gave it any thought, sir.'

'I'm sure you didn't. But there was a time, four or five thousand years ago when mankind was confined to the surface of Earth. Even then, his culture had grown quite technological and his numbers had increased to the point where any failure in technology would have meant mass starvation and disease. To maintain the technological level and advance it in the face of an increasing population, more and more technicians and scientists had to be trained, and yet, as science advanced, it took longer and longer to train them.

'As first interplanetary and then interstellar travel was developed, the problem grew more acute. In fact, actual colonization of extra-Solar planets was impossible for about fifteen hundred years because of a lack of properly trained men.

'The turning point came when the mechanics of the storage of knowledge within the brain was worked out. Once that had been done, it became possible to devise Educational tapes that would modify the mechanics in such a way as to place within the mind a body of knowledge ready-made so to speak. But you know about *that*.

'Once that was done, trained men could be turned out by the thousands and millions, and we could begin what some-one has since called the "Filling of the Universe". There are now fifteen hundred inhabited planets in the Galaxy and there is no end in sight.

'Do you see all that is involved? Earth exports Education tapes for low-specialized professions and that keeps the Galactic culture unified. For instance, the Reading tapes ensure a single language for all of us. – Don't look so surprised, other languages are possible, and in the past were used. Hundreds of them.

'Earth also exports highly specialized professionals and keeps its own population at an endurable level. Since they are shipped out in a balanced sex ratio, they act as self-reproductive units and help increase the populations on the Outworlds where an increase is needed. Furthermore, tapes and men are paid for in material which we much need and on which our economy depends. *Now* do you understand why our Education is the best way?'

'Yes, sir.'

'Does it help you to understand, knowing that without it, interstellar colonization was impossible for fifteen hundred years?'

'Yes, sir.'

'Then you see the uses of history.' The Historian smiled. 'And now I wonder if you see why I'm interested in you?'

George snapped out of time and space back to reality. Ingenescu, apparently, didn't talk aimlessly. All this lecture had been a device to attack him from a new angle.

He said, once again withdrawn, hesitating, 'Why?'

'Social Scientists work with societies and societies are made up of people.'

'All right.'

'But people aren't machines. The professionals in physical science work with machines. There is only a limited amount to know about a machine and the professionals know it all. Furthermore, all machines of a given sort are just about alike so that there is nothing to interest them in any given individual machine. But people, ah – They are so complex and so different one from another that a Social Scientist never knows all there is to know or even a good part of what there is to know. To understand his own specialty, he must always be ready to study people; particularly unusual specimens.'

'Like me,' said George tonelessly.

'I shouldn't call you a specimen, I suppose, but you are unusual. You're worth studying, and if you will allow me that privilege then, in return, I will help you if you are in trouble and if I can.'

There were pin wheels whirring in George's mind. – All this talk about people and colonization made possible by Education. It was as though caked thoughts within him were being broken up and strewn about mercilessly.

He said, 'Let me think,' and clamped his hands over his ears.

He took them away and said to the Historian, 'Will you do something for me, sir?'

'If I can,' said the Historian amiably.

'And everything I say in this room is a privileged communication. You said so.'

'And I meant it.'

'Then get me an interview with an Outworld official, with – with a Novian.'

Ingenescu looked startled. 'Well, now –'

'You can do it,' said George earnestly. 'You're an important official. I saw the policeman's look when you put that card in front of his eyes. If you refuse, I – I won't let you study me.'

It sounded a silly threat in George's own ears, one without force. On Ingenescu, however, it seemed to have a strong effect.

He said, 'That's an impossible condition. A Novian in Olympics month –'

'All right, then, get me a Novian on the phone and I'll make my own arrangements for an interview.'

'Do you think you can?'

'I know I can. Wait and see.'

Ingenescu stared at George thoughtfully and then reached for the visiphone.

George waited, half drunk with this new outlook on the whole problem and the sense of power it brought. It couldn't miss. It *couldn't* miss. He would be a Novian yet. He would leave Earth in triumph despite Antonelli and the whole crew of fools at the House for the (he almost laughed aloud) Feeble-minded.

George watched eagerly as the visiplate lit up. It would open up a window into a room of Novians, a window into a small patch of Novia transplanted to Earth. In twenty-four hours, he had accomplished that much.

There was a burst of laughter as the plate unmisted and sharpened, but for the moment no single head could be seen

148

but rather the fast passing of the shadows of men and women, this way and that. A voice was heard, clear-worded over a background of babble. 'Ingenescu? He wants me?'

Then there he was, staring out of the plate. A Novian. A genuine Novian. (George had not an atom of doubt. There was something completely Outworldly about him. Nothing that could be completely defined, or even momentarily mistaken.)

He was swarthy in complexion with a dark wave of hair combed rigidly back from his forehead. He wore a thin black moustache and a pointed beard, just as dark, that scarcely reached below the lower limit of his narrow chin, but the rest of his face was so smooth that it looked as though it had been depilated permanently.

He was smiling. 'Ladislas, this goes too far. We fully expect to be spied on, within reason, during our stay on Earth, but mind reading is out of bounds.'

'Mind reading, Honourable?'

'Confess! You knew I was going to call you this evening. You knew I was only waiting to finish this drink.' His hand moved up into view and his eye peered through a small glass of a faintly violet liqueur. 'I can't offer you one, I'm afraid.'

George, out of range of Ingenescu's transmitter, could not be seen by the Novian. He was relieved at that. He wanted time to compose himself and he needed it badly. It was as though he were made up exclusively of restless fingers, drumming, drumming –

But he was right. He hadn't miscalculated. Ingenescu *was* important. The Novian called him by his first name.

Good! Things worked well. What George had lost on Antonelli, he would make up, with advantage, on Ingenescu. And someday, when he was on his own at last, and could come back to Earth as powerful a Novian as this one who could negligently joke with Ingenescu's first name and be addressed as 'Honourable' in turn – when he came back, he would settle with Antonelli. He had a year and a half to pay back and he –

He all but lost his balance on the brink of the enticing day-dream and snapped back in sudden anxious realization that he was losing the thread of what was going on.

The Novian was saying, ' – doesn't hold water. Novia has a civilization as complicated and advanced as Earth's. We're not Zeston, after all. It's ridiculous that we have to come here for individual technicians.'

Ingenescu said soothingly, 'Only for new models. There is never any certainty that new models will be needed. To buy the Educational tapes would cost you the same price as a thousand technicians, how do you know you would need that many?'

The Novian tossed off what remained of his drink and laughed. (It displeased George, somehow, that a Novian should be this frivolous. He wondered uneasily if perhaps the Novian ought not to have skipped that drink and even the one or two before that.)

The Novian said, 'That's typical pious fraud, Ladislas. You know we can make use of all the late models we can get. I collected five Metallurgists this afternoon – '

'I know,' said Ingenescu. 'I was there.'

'Watching me! Spying!' cried the Novian. 'I'll tell you what it is. The new-model Metallurgists I got differed from the previous model only in knowing the use of Beeman Spectrographs. The tapes couldn't be modified that much, not that much' (he held up two fingers close together) 'from last year's model. You introduce the new models only to *make* us buy and spend and come here hat in hand.'

'We don't *make* you buy.'

'No, but you sell late-model technicians to Landonum and so we have to keep pace. It's a merry-go-round you have us on, you pious Earthmen, but watch out, there may be an exit somewhere.' There was a sharp edge to his laugh, and it ended sooner than it should have.

Ingenescu said, 'In all honesty, I hope there is. Meanwhile, as to the purpose of my call – '

'That's right, *you* called. Oh, well, I've said my say and I suppose next year there'll be a new model of Metallurgist anyway for us to spend goods on, probably with a new gimmick for niobium assays and nothing else altered and the next year – But go on, what is it you want?'

'I have a young man here to whom I wish you to speak.'

'Oh?' The Novian looked not completely pleased with that. 'Concerning what?'

'I can't say. He hasn't told me. For that matter he hasn't

even told me his name and profession.'

The Novian frowned. 'Then why take up my time?'

'He seems quite confident that you will be interested in what he has to say.'

'I dare say.'

'And,' said Ingenescu, 'as a favour to me.'

The Novian shrugged. 'Put him on and tell him to make it short.'

Ingenescu stepped aside and whispered to George, 'Address him as "Honourable".'

George swallowed with difficulty. This was it.

George felt himself going moist with perspiration. The thought had come so recently, yet it was in him now so certainly. The beginnings of it had come when he had spoken to Trevelyan, then everything had fermented and billowed into shape while Ingenescu had prattled, and then the Novian's own remarks had seemed to nail it all into place.

George said, 'Honourable, I've come to show you the exit from the merry-go-round.' Deliberately, he adopted the Novian's own metaphor.

The Novian stared at him gravely. 'What merry-go-round?'

'You yourself mentioned it, Honourable. The merry-go-round that Novia is on when you come to Earth to – to get technicians.' (He couldn't keep his teeth from chattering; from excitement, not fear.)

The Novian said, 'You're trying to say that you know a way by which we can avoid patronizing Earth's mental super-market. Is that it?'

'Yes, sir. You can control your own Educational system.'

'Umm. Without tapes?'

'Y – yes, Honourable.'

The Novian, without taking his eyes from George, called out, 'Ingenescu, get into view.'

The Historian moved to where he could be seen over George's shoulder.

The Novian said, 'What is this? I don't seem to penetrate.'

'I assure you solemnly,' said Ingenescu, 'that whatever this is it is being done on the young man's own initiative, Honourable. I have not inspired this. I have nothing to do with it.'

'Well, then, what is the young man to you? Why do you call me on his behalf?'

Ingenescu said, 'He is an object of study, Honourable. He has value to me and I humour him.'

'What kind of value?'

'It's difficult to explain; a matter of my profession.'

The Novian laughed shortly. 'Well, to each his profession.' He nodded to an invisible person or persons outside plate range. 'There's a young man here, a protégé of Ingenescu or some such thing, who will explain to us how to Educate without tapes.' He snapped his fingers, and another glass of pale liqueur appeared in his hand. 'Well, young man?'

The faces on the plate were multiple now. Men and women, both, crammed in for a view of George, their faces moulded into various shades of amusement and curiosity.

George tried to look disdainful. They were all, in their own ways, Novians as well as the Earthman, 'studying' him as though he were a bug on a pin. Ingenescu was sitting in a corner, now, watching him owl-eyed.

Fools, he thought tensely, one and all. But they would have to understand. He would *make* them understand.

He said, 'I was at the Metallurgist Olympics this afternoon.'

'You, too?' said the Novian blandly. 'It seems all Earth was there.'

'No, Honourable, but I was. I had a friend who competed and who made out very badly because you were using the Beeman machines. His Education had included only the Henslers, apparently an older model. You said the modification involved was slight.' George held up two fingers close together in conscious mimicry of the other's previous gesture. 'And my friend had known some time in advance that knowledge of the Beeman machines would be required.'

'And what does that signify?'

'It was my friend's lifelong ambition to qualify for Novia. He already knew the Henslers. He had to know the Beemans to qualify and he knew that. To learn about the Beemans would have taken just a few more facts, a bit more data, a small amount of practice perhaps. With a life's ambition riding the scale, he might have managed this – '

'And where would he have obtained a tape for the additional

facts and data? Or has Education become a private matter for home study here on Earth?'

There was dutiful laughter from the faces in the background.

George said, 'That's why he didn't learn, Honourable. He thought he needed a tape. He wouldn't even try without one, no matter what the prize. He refused to try without a tape.'

'Refused, eh? Probably the type of fellow who would refuse to fly without a skimmer.' More laughter and the Novian thawed into a smile and said, 'The fellow is amusing. Go on. I'll give you another few moments.'

George said tensely, 'Don't think this is a joke. Tapes are actually bad. They teach too much; they're too painless. A man who learns that way doesn't know how to learn any other way. He's frozen into whatever position he's been taped. Now if a person *weren't* given tapes but were forced to learn by hand, so to speak, from the start; why, then he'd get the habit of learning, and continue to learn. Isn't that reasonable? Once he has the habit well developed he can be given just a small amount of tape-knowledge, perhaps, to fill in gaps or fix details. Then he can make further progress on his own. You can make Beeman Metallurgists out of your own Hensler Metallurgists in that way and not have to come to Earth for new models.'

The Novian nodded and sipped at his drink. 'And where does everyone get knowledge without tapes? From interstellar vacuum?'

'From books. By studying the instruments themselves. By *thinking*.'

'Books? How does one understand books without Education?'

'Books are in words. Words can be understood for the most part. Specialized words can be explained by the technicians you already have.'

'What about Reading? Will you allow Reading tapes?'

'Reading tapes are all right, I suppose, but there's no reason you can't learn to read the old way, too. At least in part.'

The Novian said, 'So that you can develop good habits from the start?'

'Yes, yes,' George said gleefully. The man was beginning to understand.

'And what about mathematics?'

'That's the easiest of all, sir – Honourable. Mathematics is different from other technical subjects. It starts with certain simple principles and proceeds by steps. You can start with nothing and learn. It's practically designed for that. Then, once you know the proper types of mathematics, other technical books become quite understandable. Especially if you start with easy ones.'

'Are there easy books?'

'Definitely. Even if there weren't, the technicians you now have can try to write easy books. Some of them might be able to put some of their knowledge into words and symbols.'

'Good Lord,' said the Novian to the men clustered about him. 'The young devil has an answer for everything.'

'I have. I have,' shouted George. 'Ask me.'

'Have you tried learning from books yourself? Or is this just theory with you?'

George turned to look quickly at Ingenescu, but the Historian was passive. There was no sign of anything but gentle interest in his face.

George said, 'I have.'

'And do you find it works?'

'Yes, Honourable,' said George eagerly. 'Take me with you to Novia. I can set up a programme and direct – '

'Wait, I have a few more questions. How long would it take, do you suppose, for you to become a Metallurgist capable of handling a Beeman machine, supposing you started from nothing and did not use Educational tapes?'

George hesitated. 'Well – years, perhaps.'

'Two years? Five? Ten?'

'I can't say, Honourable.'

'Well, there's a vital question to which you have no answer, have you? Shall we say five years? Does that sound reasonable to you?'

'I suppose so.'

'All right. We have a technician studying metallurgy according to this method of yours for five years. He's no good to us during that time, you'll admit, but he must be fed and housed and paid all that time.'

154

'But – '

'Let me finish. Then when he's done and can use the Beeman, five years have passed. Don't you suppose we'll have modified Beemans then which he *won't* be able to use?'

'But by then he'll be expert on learning. He could learn the new details necessary in a matter of days.'

'So you say. And suppose this friend of yours, for instance, had studied up on Beemans on his own and managed to learn it; would he be as expert in its use as a competitor who had learned it off the tapes?'

'Maybe not – ' began George.

'Ah,' said the Novian.

'Wait, let *me* finish. Even if he doesn't know something as well, it's the ability to learn further that's important. He may be able to think up things, new things that no tape-Educated man would. You'll have a reservoir of original thinkers – '

'In your studying,' said the Novian, 'have you thought up any new things?'

'No, but I'm just one man and I haven't studied long – '

'Yes. – Well, ladies, gentlemen, have we been sufficiently amused?'

'Wait,' cried George, in sudden panic. 'I want to arrange a personal interview. There are things I can't explain over the visiphone. There are details – '

The Novian looked past George. 'Ingenescu! I think I have done you your favour. Now, really, I have a heavy schedule tomorrow. Be well!'

The screen went blank.

George's hands shot out towards the screen, as though in a wild impulse to shake life back into it. He cried out, 'He didn't believe me. He didn't believe me.'

Ingenescu said, 'No, George. Did you really think he would?'

George scarcely heard him. 'But why not? It's all true. It's all so much to his advantage. No risk. I and a few men to work with – A dozen men training for years would cost less than one technician. – He was drunk! Drunk! He didn't understand.'

George looked about breathlessly. 'How do I get to him? I've got to. This was wrong. Shouldn't have used the visiphone.

I need time. Face to face. How do I – '

Ingenescu said, 'He won't see you, George. And if he did, he wouldn't believe you.'

'He will, I tell you. When he isn't drinking. He – ' George turned squarely towards the Historian and his eyes widened. 'Why do you call me George?'

'Isn't that your name? George Platen?'

'You know me?'

'All about you.'

George was motionless except for the breath pumping his chest wall up and down.

Ingenescu said, 'I want to help you, George. I told you that. I've been studying you and I want to help you.'

George screamed. 'I don't need help. I'm not feeble-minded. The whole world is, but I'm not.' He whirled and dashed madly for the door.

He flung it open and two policemen roused themselves suddenly from their guard duty and seized him.

For all George's straining, he could feel the hypo-spray at the fleshy point just under the corner of his jaw, and that was it. The last thing he remembered was the face of Ingenescu, watching with gentle concern.

George opened his eyes to the whiteness of a ceiling. He remembered what had happened. He remembered it distantly as though it had happened to somebody else. He stared at the ceiling till the whiteness filled his eyes and washed his brain clean, leaving room, it seemed, for new thought and new ways of thinking.

He didn't know how long he lay there so, listening to the drift of his own thinking.

There was a voice in his ear. 'Are you awake?'

And George heard his own moaning for the first time. Had he been moaning? He tried to turn his head.

The voice said, 'Are you in pain, George?'

George whispered, 'Funny. I was so anxious to leave Earth. I didn't understand.'

'Do you know where you are?'

'Back in the – the House.' George managed to turn. The voice belonged to Omani.

George said, 'It's funny I didn't understand.'

Omani smiled gently. 'Sleep again – '

George slept.

And woke again. His mind was clear.

Omani sat at the bedside reading, but he put down the book as George's eyes opened.

George struggled to a sitting position. He said, 'Hello.'

'Are you hungry?'

'You bet.' He stared at Omani curiously. 'I was followed when I left, wasn't I?'

Omani nodded. 'You were under observation at all times. We were going to manoeuvre you to Antonelli and let you discharge your aggressions. We felt that to be the only way you could make progress. Your emotions were clogging your advance.'

George said, with a trace of embarrassment, 'I was all wrong about him.'

'It doesn't matter now. When you stopped to stare at the Metallurgy notice board at the airport, one of our agents reported back the list of names. You and I had talked about your past sufficiently so that I caught the significance of Trevelyan's name there. You asked for directions to the Olympics; there was the possibility that this might result in the kind of crisis we were hoping for; we sent Ladislas Ingenescu to the hall to meet you and take over.'

'He's an important man in the government, isn't he?'

'Yes, he is.'

'And you had him take over. It makes me sound important.'

'You *are* important, George.'

A thick stew had arrived, steaming, fragrant. George grinned wolfishly and pushed his sheets back to free his arms. Omani helped arrange the bed-table. For a while, George ate silently.

Then George said, 'I woke up here once before just for a short time.'

Omani said, 'I know. I was here.'

'Yes, I remember. You know, everything was changed. It was as though I was too tired to feel emotion. I wasn't angry any more. I could just think. It was as though I had been drugged to wipe out emotion.'

'You weren't,' said Omani. 'Just sedation. You had rested.'

'Well, anyway, it was all clear to me, as though I had known it all the time but wouldn't listen to myself. I thought: What was it I had wanted Novia to let me do? I had wanted to go to Novia and take a batch of un-Educated youngsters and teach them out of books. I had wanted to establish a House for the Feeble-minded – like here – and Earth already has them – many of them.'

Omani's white teeth gleamed as he smiled. 'The Institute of Higher Studies is the correct name for places like this.'

'Now I see it,' said George, 'so easily I am amazed at my blindness before. After all, who invents the new instrument models that require new-model technicians? Who invented the Beeman spectrographs, for instance? A man called Beeman, I suppose, but he couldn't have been tape-Educated or how could he have made the advance?'

'Exactly.'

'Or who makes Educational tapes? Special tape-making technicians? Then who makes the tapes to train *them*? More advanced technicians? Then who makes the tapes – You see what I mean. Somewhere there has to be an end. Somewhere there must be men and women with capacity for original thought.'

'Yes, George.'

George leaned back, stared over Omani's head, and for a moment there was the return of something like restlessness to his eyes.

'Why wasn't I told all this at the beginning?'

'Oh, if we could,' said Omani, 'the trouble it would save us. We can analyse a mind, George, and say this one will make an adequate architect and that one a good wood-worker. We know of no way of detecting the capacity for original, creative thought. It is too subtle a thing. We have some rule-of-thumb methods that mark out individuals who may possibly or potentially have such a talent.

'On Reading Day, such individuals are reported. You were, for instance. Roughly speaking, the number so reported comes to one in ten thousand. By the time Education Day arrives, these individuals are checked again, and nine out of ten of them turn out to have been false alarms. Those who remain are sent to places like this.'

George said, 'Well, what's wrong with telling people that one out of – of a hundred thousand will end at places like these? Then it won't be such a shock to those who do.'

'And those who don't? The ninety-nine thousand nine hundred and ninety-nine that don't? We can't have all those people considering themselves failures. They aim at the professions and one way or another they all make it. Everyone can place after his or her name: Registered something-or-other. In one fashion or another every individual has his or her place in society and this is necessary.'

'But we?' said George. 'The one in ten thousand exception?'

'You can't be told. That's exactly it. It's the final test. Even after we've thinned out the possibilities on Education Day, nine out of ten of those who come here are not quite the material of creative genius, and there's no way we can distinguish those nine from the tenth that we want by any form of machinery. The tenth one must tell us himself.'

'How?'

'We bring you here to a House for the Feeble-minded and the man who won't accept that is the man we want. It's a method that can be cruel, but it works. It won't do to say to a man, "You can create. Do so." It is much safer to wait for a man to say, "I can create, and I will do so whether you wish it or not." There are ten thousand men like you, George, who support the advancing technology of fifteen hundred worlds. We can't allow ourselves to miss one recruit to that number or waste our efforts on one member who doesn't measure up.'

George pushed his empty plate out of the way and lifted a cup of coffee to his lips.

'What about the people here who don't – measure up?'

'They are taped eventually and become our Social Scientists. Ingenescu is one. I am a Registered Psychologist. We are second echelon, so to speak.'

George finished his coffee. He said, 'I still wonder about one thing.'

'What is that?'

George threw aside the sheet and stood up. 'Why do they call them Olympics?'